BREAKING
FREE

WINTER PAGE

WITHDRAWN

Harmony Ink

Published by
Harmony Ink Press
5032 Capital Circle SW
Suite 2, PMB# 279
Tallahassee, FL 32305-7886
USA
publisher@harmonyinkpress.com
http://harmonyinkpress.com

Breaking Free
© 2014 Winter Page.

Cover Art
© 2014 L.C. Chase.
http://www.lcchase.com
Cover content is for illustrative purposes only
and any person depicted on the cover is a model.

ISBN: 978-1-62798-914-5
Library ISBN: 978-1-62798-916-9
Digital ISBN: 978-1-62798-915-2

Printed in the United States of America
First Edition
April 2014

Library Edition
July 2014

For Drake. Thank you.

ONE

IN A way, my parents' utter stupidity when they named me was a blessing. It's a lot easier for people to get the memo that you're a girl when you've been called Raimi all your life. But then again, it was a total pain in the ass to get the gender on my driver's license changed.

I was one of those boys born to look a little like a girl. I'd like to say it was my lush chocolate hair. Or maybe it was just that my mom's attractive genes had played unusually dominant. Either way, it made facial surgery pretty straightforward. No nose jobs for me, just some minor nip and tucks and a touch of laser hair removal. Gotta love modern day technology, right?

I sighed, my shoulders settling restlessly. I tried smiling in my car's mirror and redid my lip gloss. It was my first day of high school in Little, Connecticut. More to the point, my first day of real high school. Although I was going to be a junior this year, I'd been homeschooled back in Texas. Which meant that I was as terrified as any freshman on their first day of high school with the big kids.

Satisfied with my makeup, or at least resigned to this being as good as it got, I slowly opened my door. It was a bigger relief than I had thought it would be, knowing that this was a fresh start. No one would question it when I went to the girl's bathroom. No one would even know I started life out as a boy. That fact alone gave me the strength to walk through those ominous, craptastically tacky orange doors.

1

I don't know what I expected from a brick-and-mortar high school, but this wasn't it. I guess I imagined a preppy, pristine populous with their ties tied and skirts perfectly pleated, or maybe a postapocalyptic jungle of horny animals. Instead, it was just normal kids, age fourteen to eighteen. Completely ordinary.

Some of the girls gave me narrowed stares, and I smiled to myself. It was one thing for people to finally see me as a girl, but it was something else entirely to be seen as actual female *competition.* I had to stifle a laugh when the jocks turned to watch me walk by like I was a shiny new toy.

I knew I was pretty by girl standards. I mean I had a really good surgeon that we had paid to make me pretty. Except it had never been about being an attractive girl. It was about getting into the body that fit my real gender. But that didn't mean today's stares weren't flattering.

I glanced down at my schedule and navigated to my first class. AP Spanish. Ugh. Not the best way to start the morning, but I supposed it could be a lot worse. It could have been chemistry.

When I entered the Spanish classroom, the kids already there looked up at me in confusion. "You're not a senior," a muscle-bound blond boy from the back announced.

Wow. A real Einstein, there. I nodded at him, smirking a little despite myself. It was good to know that the football players at least met my expectation in their polyester-and-pleather varsity jackets and semiliterate English. I strode across the room, readjusting the strap on my book bag.

"Hello, Mrs. Gonzales, I'm Raimi Carter, the new girl from Texas," I murmured softly.

She beamed at me from her desk and rushed to shake my hand. "Raimi! Oh, it's such a pleasure to meet you! It's been so long since Clark has had a new student. Estoy deseando tener a un estudiante talentoso en mi clase. He oído que tu madre te enseñó bastante en Texas," she gushed, her accent absolutely perfect. Translation—I look forward to having such a gifted student in my classroom. I hear your mother taught you quite a bit back in Texas.

It was clear she would be a sweet teacher who cheered for all her students to learn and graded easy, and that wasn't a bad thing. I nodded and said as correctly and quickly as I could, "Me encanta el idioma, es tan hermoso. Y sí, mi madre fue criada en España y me enseñó muy bien. Espero continuar con mi aprendizaje." Translation—I love the language. It's so beautiful. And yes, my mother was raised in Spain and taught me very well. I look forward to continuing my learning.

The teacher's eyes lit up. It was obvious she hadn't expected me to be quite so fluent. I could almost hear my mother laughing, refusing to speak English to me until I got the accent marks right on a grammar exercise or the pronunciation perfect on a particularly challenging word.

Mrs. Gonzales shuffled through several piles of paper on her desk until I had all the handouts that she would call on as resources in class.

I silently slid into a seat on the back row, abruptly tired of being stared at. I sat, toying with my necklace until the bell rang and class began. After about five minutes of a lecture I had already learned last year, I tuned out and started doodling in my journal.

When the homework was passed out, I finished the simple worksheet at light speed and leaned back in my chair to observe the room. I literally could not describe how anticlimactic it was.

I was struck by the sad, bland, white-bread color of everyone's faces. I glanced down at my own caramel skin, inherited from my Spanish mother. My mom's people came from the south coast of Spain. Sailors and pirates from southern Europe, Africa, and the Middle East had spread their genetics pretty freely in that part of the world for many centuries. I figure I'm more or less a mutt. A *different* looking mutt.

I had never gotten a sunburn in my life. I just tanned darker until I was a creamy caramel, and then my skin just decided to give up and stay that color. I was short for a boy and tall for a girl, maybe five foot six on a good day. I had long, dark brown hair and thick eyelashes to match. My hair was naturally really wavy, but I straightened it most every morning. My face was more heart-shaped in structure than anything else. I had a thin nose, and my lips were full like my grandmother's. Not much different about all of that, right? But my eyes, they were what made my face. They were like honey, warm and golden.

When most people first saw me, they just stared at my eyes, confused. Or maybe they were trying to see the lines of contacts. Except there were none, much to the chagrin of skeptical onlookers. My mom always told me that it was my inner beauty coming from my heart that made people stare, but I honestly thought it was the weird mix of my corn-fed Iowa boy of a dad and the exotic, fierce, almost catlike looks my mom had been blessed with. Lost in my thoughts, I jumped when the bell signaling the end of class chimed obnoxiously over the loudspeaker.

I gathered my things and rushed out the door, eager to get to my next class. Math was my absolute favorite subject of all time. It was embarrassing, but numbers always made sense to me.

When I first started gender transitioning, my mother had been the most supportive parent of all time. She pulled me from school and taught me from home for two years so that I could be myself in peace. She'd gotten a master's in education before she went to law school, and I sincerely believed she was the smartest person I had ever met. She brought in tutors to teach *her* what I needed to learn, and then she taught me.

Her big spiel on sacrificing her normal career and social life for me was that she loved me, and love is love. She gave me the best education I could have hoped for; therefore, I was in all senior AP courses in this school as a junior. Of course, going to this school was more about learning the ropes of teenage society and interactions from a girl's point of view.

My mom hoped that life for all of us would be blissfully uneventful in this small town. So did I.

Truly, I wasn't expecting anything big, anything revolutionary or life changing in my human experience to happen in the next two years. Imagine my surprise, then, when I walked into the AP Calculus class and saw arguably the most beautiful girl I had ever laid eyes on. She literally stopped me in my tracks.

She had that whole windswept, Farrah Fawcett thing going on with her long flaxen hair. She had fair, flawless skin, the blonde girl equivalent to mine. Her legs were crossed beneath a tiny skirt, her limbs seeming to go on for miles and miles of tanned muscle tone. I was lucky enough to walk in as she was laughing, her toothpaste-commercial smile lighting up the entire room.

But her *eyes*.

I swear they were like turquoise, that same blue-green sparking like flint and steel across the room. I stared at her the entire way to the teacher's desk. I handed the wheezing old man my transcript, and he mechanically handed me papers. Seeing her was like looking at the sun for too long. I took a seat in the far back of the room, trying not to make my amazement overly obvious. I didn't even think she had seen me. Unfortunately, my complete, budding hero-worship was interrupted by the dreaded bell.

The old man stood, his knees popping like giant knuckles. He shuffled over to his podium and leaned heavily on it. He didn't even bother smiling. His deep voice just boomed out to address us.

"Welcome to hell, my unsuspecting victims. There will be pop quizzes, and there will be homework every night. Get used to it because life doesn't get any easier. That said, I will treat all of you fairly and try to teach each and every one of you the material to the best of my ability. Now, I would like everyone to introduce himself or herself," he droned.

A glint of humor in his eyes told me he meant every word he'd said, but that he was a cool guy beneath it all and a confident teacher.

No doubt about it. I was going to absolutely love this class, even if he gave lots of work. He nodded at a boy in the front row, who I'm pretty sure was stoned, to start us out.

Everybody said their names like good little children, until the boy sitting behind the prettiest girl on earth. He smirked like the asshole I knew instinctively that he must be and said, "My name is the Beast." His voice was deep and flat like a dead fish.

It was good to know that the people around me were genuinely ridiculous. It made me feel a little better about myself, at least.

The beauty just rolled her eyes and said in a soft, sultry voice, "I'm Clare Strickland. Otherwise known as the Beast's girlfriend."

I thought I was going to fall out of my chair. It was like someone had knocked the breath out of me. But a) she was taken; and b) she had a boyfriend who could obviously stick his fist through a brick wall and not flinch. Sigh. Oh well.

I waited my turn to speak and said obediently, "I'm Raimi." I hoped my voice was loud enough for Clare to hear.

She raised a perfectly shaped eyebrow at me and said lightly, "Raimi? No offense, but where did your parents get that?"

The class laughed. I shrugged. "Story of my life, hon."

She laughed then, throwing her hair back. I heard some snickers from the back at my use of "hon." I didn't care, though, because it made Clare laugh.

The rest of the day was horribly uneventful, going by about as fast as molasses. During my study hall, I had to pick up a few textbooks I was missing, which brought me down the school's wide front hallway. My beat up Converses squeaked on the linoleum as I approached the attendance office.

When the woman there looked up at me from behind the glass window, she broke into a tentative smile. She slid back the glass window to talk with me. "Hello, dear. What can I help you with?"

"I need to get some textbooks I'm missing. Is there somewhere I should go or someone I should talk to?" I asked.

She nodded, pointing down the hallway in the opposite direction of the entrance.

"Just go down that hall until it ends and turn left. The book room is the first door on the right. Grab the books you need and fill out one of the sign-out forms in the folder hanging inside the door. Bring that to me. You'll turn the books in at the same place at the end of the year. Is there anything else?"

I shook my head and turned down the long hallway. I gazed up at the ceiling, counting the ceiling tiles as I went. Each of them was painted, an art project I'm sure had taken hours and hours to complete. When I turned left, the decorated tiles ended. I wondered what would get painted on the blank tiles once it was their turn to be covered in too-bright acrylics. They were kind of like me. I had once been decorated one way—garish and clumsy. Now I had a fresh coat of white paint on my life, waiting once more for a story to be painted upon it.

I turned the door handle slowly and peered into the dusty stacks of dustier textbooks. Quietly, I made my way through row after row of books. I found everything except for the Art History book I needed.

I still don't know what made me turn down that particular row marked Science and Tech, but I'm glad I did. I stopped midstep, hushed voices reaching my ears from the next row over.

"Brad, I really don't want to." Clare's voice was recognizable, even in its cautious whisper. It had a silky quality to it that I couldn't have forgotten if I tried. I crept forward, trying to hear better.

"Aw c'mon, baby. Just a quickie?" Beast said. Although I'd heard at lunch that his name was actually Brad.

My nose squinched up in distaste. I heard a shuffling of books and then small noises of protest. That was when I decided to make my presence known. I circled back and walked into the mouth of their row, Humanities, trying to look completely involved with the titles of books.

I squeaked in surprise and murmured, "Oh, um, sorry, I didn't know you two were back here. Um, you wouldn't happen to know where the Art History textbooks are, would you?" I stumbled, honestly surprised by the scene.

Brad had Clare arched backward over a low, wheeled book cart, his hand dangerously high on her thigh. The look he gave me, well, I honestly thought he would growl at me in a testosterone-induced rage and charge me. He straightened slowly, and I thought that maybe I heard him growl under his breath.

Clare looked sick with fear as she wiped the corner of her mouth where her lipstick had smeared, lowering herself off the top shelf of the cart and tugging her skirt back down where it belonged. I noticed her surreptitiously pushing Brad's hand off of her leg as she pointed in the other direction from me.

"Art History is down that way, last shelf on the right, eye level." Her voice quavered badly.

I tried to shake the unease churning in my stomach and pasted on a big smile. "Thanks!" And with that, I rushed past them to get my textbook. I heard them leave and hurried out behind them. I just wanted to go home and try to forget what I had seen.

High school was nothing like what I thought it would be.

TWO

ONCE I got home, I grabbed an apple, went upstairs to my room, and started my homework. I was used to being productive in the house, so in a matter of about thirty minutes, I had done all my Physics, all my Calc, and the draft of my Lit essay that wasn't due until Friday.

In other words, I spent most of the night staring at the ceiling of my room, listening to music, and thinking. Sometimes having no social life was the most relaxing thing in the world. It was lonely, though, and I'm not ashamed to admit that.

Completely bored, I went into the bathroom. Like the brat I was, I looked at my body, trying to find curves I hadn't seen before. I still had to take female hormone injections, but I was down to one a week.

All my life, I had been stuck with a stupidly fast metabolism, one that a lot of people would kill for. But you have no idea what I would do to fill out my hips a little more, just so I could look more like a *girl*.

Back at my old school in Texas, I used to watch girls literally starve themselves, and it made me so angry. The only thing I could think was, don't you know that's what makes you a girl, for God's sake! Of course, I had a lot to be angry about, back then. It's an epically raw deal to be born into the wrong body.

Sighing, I went back into my room and proceeded to sleep for an hour, only to awake to the tangy scent of Chinese takeout.

I trudged into the family dining room, expecting and receiving chaos. I went over to our kitchen counter and served myself a little of everything my mom had ordered from work and had delivered here for us. I sat down at the family table, eating in silence. Eventually, my little brother, Zach, bounded in, his blond hair tousled from the headset he wore when he played video games. I'm telling you, the little guy was a complete hot mess. He was seven and the spitting image of my dad.

I laughed and grabbed him in his pursuit of food. Squealing with laughter, he tried to squirm away as I tickled him.

"What's wrong, Zach-o? Something bothering you?" I teased, flipping him upside down and dangling him from his ankles. His straight hair hung from his head, and he continued to laugh manically.

Finally, he opened his blue eyes and smiled up at me. "Yes! You're bothering me, silly!" he shouted excitedly, enjoying every minute of this.

I threw him up the way I always did, and he landed on his feet, just like he did every time we played. The lucky thing about our age difference was that it was nine years, so I knew how to be independent, and he never really got in my way or annoyed me. I never did understand how siblings could be so hostile. Although, if he was two or three years behind me, that might be a different story.

I smiled as he served himself a huge mountain of fried rice, just in time for my mom to get home from her law firm. She had set up a new practice since we moved to Little, and it had been absolute chaos for the past month as more and more people discovered that a Harvard-educated lawyer had come to town. When I saw the bags under her eyes, I didn't try to conceal my worry.

"How's work, Mama?" Zach asked through a mouthful of rice.

My mom smiled, ruffling his hair. "It's great. I just got another major client today, so business is booming." Her voice lit up as she chatted with him about his first day of school. She filled her plate and sat down with us at the table, almost like a traditional family supper. Almost.

I was glad to see that she perked up a little as she ate. We all talked about new teachers and homework and the other kids, and it was all very, very normal.

For the first time since my sixth-grade year, this annual conversation wasn't fraught with tension and unspoken worry about my not fitting in, bullying, and whether or not I'd had any thoughts of harming myself. Thank God Zach was too little to remember any of that. I hoped he was too little to understand most of what I'd been through over the past few years. Although in fairness to my folks, they'd been through a lot with me, too.

I had just stood up to put my plate in the sink when I heard the back door open and close. My dad was home. My entire middle clenched, and suddenly, the Chinese food felt heavy and pasty in my stomach. Zach kept eating, completely unbothered. My mom just gave me a sympathetic look we both understood.

Hurriedly, I rinsed off my plate and was sprinting up the stairs when I heard his deep voice boom from behind me. "And where do you think you're going? I just got home and want a hug!" he slurred, his speech unsteady.

I rolled my eyes. My dad was a great businessman whenever he wasn't smashed. Which wasn't very often. I turned around slowly and headed back down, one reluctant step at a time. When I reached the second one from the bottom, I was crushed in a bear hug. He was a big man, my dad, easily six foot four and about 280 pounds.

I squeaked, my air cut off. "Dad. Can't breathe."

He laughed boisterously and let me go.

I smiled lamely, smelling the gin on his breath. "Nice to see you, Dad. I'm going to go do my homework, now." I tried not to clench my teeth too hard when I said it. It wasn't that I hated my dad or that he'd done anything really bad to me. We were just as different as two human beings could be.

He laughed and said, "Good for you, son, good for you." He nodded and then turned and walked away, weaving his way toward the kitchen.

I tried not to let the word "son" bother me too much. He was very drunk, so I probably should be deeply flattered that he hadn't confused me with a stop sign. That didn't keep me from running up the stairs two at a time, though.

11

THE FIRST week of high school flew by in a blur of new names and faces all jumbled together like one massive soup bowl of hormonal psychopaths. I might be exaggerating a little. Everyone was nice, really. Well, all of the juniors, at least.

The seniors I was in classes with seemed to fall into one of two categories. They were either sex-driven crazy people who tried to hump everything and everyone, or they were really sweet but couldn't actually exert the effort to give one single crap about anything. The latter were the crowd I tried to get partnered up with.

But I really liked the junior class. They were loud and vulgar and a ton of fun, overall.

Luckily, I ended up managing to hang out at lunch for a couple of days in a row with the people I loved. My people. The drifter-artist types. Because here's the thing. Everyone our age was completely and utterly crazy.

It was just about picking the brand of crazy I gravitated to and the type of crazy I didn't mind submerging myself in. I've always been an artist. I actually think I drew things before I spoke my first words. And artists have always had a special place in my heart because we're the kind of people who can talk about color distribution and brush stroking technique for hours. I loved it. I absolutely loved it.

But it was a complete surprise, the first Friday of school, when my lunch table of cool artist friends suddenly broke out talking about that night's varsity football game.

I smiled carefully, not wanting to weigh in too much. All my childhood I had played peewee football, and I had been a first-string safety all through middle school. I might just possibly be a tad bit bitter over the entire affair of organized sports and the challenges they imposed on kids like me.

As I picked at my salad, Cam, a petite brunette with a talent for comic art, dragged me down the hellhole that was high school football. "Raimi, you have to go to the game tonight. It's even a home game, so you have no excuse. So help me God, I will drive over to your heavily fortified household, break in, tie you up with duct tape, and drag your immobilized ass to the bleachers. And once we get there, I'm painting your face Raider orange."

I rolled my eyes, laughing softly. The campus joke had to do with the absolutely atrocious burnt-convenience-store-candle orange we Raiders wore with pride and zeal. I shook my head in the negative, not wanting to engage.

And then of course Freddie, who was practically joined at the hip to Cam, said with a cute scowl on his chipmunk-cheeked baby face, "Don't invoke the face paint. You know that hurts us more than it hurts her."

Cam hit him on the arm playfully. I laughed as they flirted with each other and horsed around at the table. They assured all of us they were like siblings, and in fact, they had known each other practically from the uterus. But everyone knew they had a thing. I still hadn't figured out if they actually were aware of having a thing or not. But it was as obvious as a hand in front of my face.

Cam didn't let Freddie distract her, though. She zeroed in on me once more. "Oh, I'm invoking the face paint, girlfriend. Going to the game is that serious. Raimi has to experience the sacred ritual of high school football, therefore, I will be at your house at six tonight. Remind me again where you live?" Cam demanded.

I toyed with my lettuce. "How about I meet you there?" I said, not looking up from my food. I could hear the collective sigh from the table, but no one protested. I let a small smile play over my lips. I was going to my first high school football game with a group of artists who all accepted me. It was everything I had wanted. Of course, the fall hadn't come yet, and that was where life got interesting.

HIGH SCHOOL football games were a lot like a buffet. Lots of things to look at and examine, like plays on the football field or the cute girl from the opposing school. But at the same time, everything has a common factor in it, some theme that connected all of the dishes together. What united my school was our hatred of the Tigers from across town. Freddie didn't have to explain the dynamics of a burning rivalry. I had grown up in Texas where football was the state religion, and all of the people were humble servants to an oblong ball and stadiums that seated twenty thousand.

It didn't take us very long to find our seats high up in the bleachers. I glanced around, trying to figure out if the intoxication of choice was weed or booze. Scowling, I decided it was a pretty even tie.

Voicing my concern, I asked, "So is everyone always this hammered at football games?"

Cam laughed uproariously. "Oh, sweetie. It's a Friday night tradition that everyone gets completely trashed." She added casually, "I'd get used to it sooner rather than later if I were you."

I shrugged, not wanting or needing to know more.

The game went relatively quickly, the score 49 to 7 at the half. It was nice watching our state champion team decimate everything that stood in their steroid-enhanced way. Everyone was up and stretching at halftime when I noticed something disturbing on the sideline. Clare was walking off the field with Brad, her cheerleading skirt swaying as she walked. Brad had his arm over her, and to anyone who just glanced at them, it would seem completely normal. But as I squinted against the glare of the stadium lights, I saw the indentions his fingers made on her shoulder and the rigid way she kept trying to push him off.

"So, Cam, what's the deal with Clare and Brad? He seems a little… aggressive," I said flippantly.

Shauna, a girl I had just met tonight, piped up, "I hear he has blackmail pics of her, so she's not leaving. Or something like that. But everyone says he has something on her the rest of the school doesn't know about. Why do you ask?" Her voice implied she was expecting a good story from me.

"I don't know. He just seems a little rapey for my taste. I'm not the one dating him, though, so it's not really my problem," I mumbled, throwing my hands up.

14

No one even looked up at me when I said that. Brad and Clare seemed to be old news and not worth spending more time on, or else everyone was done trying to get them to break up or at least to figure out if something really bad was going on.

The rest of the night was a blur of touchdown after touchdown for the Raiders, a total blowout of our Tiger rivals. Before I left, I gave Cam and Freddie my phone number so they could let me know about a supposed party the following night. I doubted I would go, considering I hadn't been invited, but I nonetheless pasted on a big smile of fake enthusiasm.

What really struck me that night, though, was watching from my car as Brad backed Clare against a wall after the game. I knew I should've gotten out. I should've done something, *anything*. But I didn't. I drove away, not turning around to watch her slap him. I definitely didn't see the glint of fury in his eyes in my rearview mirror, or imagine the threatening words I spied him whispering fiercely in her ears. And I definitely didn't see the fear take over her beautiful features, turning her paler than ice.

I SLEPT in late on Saturday after staying up all night reading. I shuffled downstairs and put my mom's pancakes in the microwave to heat up. I was rummaging around in our cabinets for syrup when my phone buzzed loudly, making me jump.

Hey babe! Party tonight, will pick you up at 8.

I sighed. Cam insisted on calling me babe, despite Freddie's and my objections. I started typing a reply when a horrifying thought crossed my mind.

Sounds great. Except I have nothing to wear.

I pinched the bridge of my nose. The one thing I hadn't expected once I started transitioning was all the time and effort I had to put into dressing myself every morning in something attractive. Makeup had been no problem. Hell, it was the easiest part. Hair had been harder to master, but I'd gotten the hang of it, eventually. But what to wear… not my strong point. My phone buzzed loudly.

Think slut and you can't go wrong.

I practically threw my phone on the floor in frustration. The sluttiest thing I owned was a peasant blouse that my grandmother *might* have called low-cut. I groaned, my pancakes forgotten for the moment. I checked the time. My mom would be in a meeting with her new client by now. I knew what I had to do. And it wasn't going to be pleasant.

My impulse was to sweet-talk my dad like the girl I now was. But he was still only marginally on board with acknowledging me as a girl. I never knew if I should suck up to him by punching his arm or kissing his cheek and saying "pretty please."

"Dad?" I murmured, peeking awkwardly into his huge study. Books lined every wall, crammed with everything from ancient texts on architecture to his business records. He was sitting in his leather armchair, reading what looked to be a book on Arabic culture in the fifteenth century. He snapped the book shut, his eyes alert and intent on me.

"What can I do for ya, champ?" he asked jovially. I smiled hesitantly. It wasn't often that I got to see the sober man my father chose to be from time to time.

"I was wondering if I could borrow your credit card to go shopping today? Nothing major. I just need to get something to wear to a party tonight." I spoke carefully, trying not to say anything that would trigger his inner conservative to have an aneurism.

"Don't you have something to wear to a party up in that closet of yours?" he asked, frowning.

I shook my head, laughing a little. "No, everything I own is a little too… classy… for a party like this." I was glad to see little wrinkles form around his eyes. Those were laugh lines and not his disapproving scowl. I'd chosen my approach correctly for once.

He chuckled deeply and rummaged around in his wallet. "All right, all right. Just nothing too out there, okay?" He could play the role of concerned parent pretty well when he wasn't doing his rendition of stumbling drunk.

I snorted. "Please, Dad. I'm not a whore. Yet." I winked, taking the credit card from his outstretched hand. He rubbed his face tiredly as I turned to leave.

"You're going to make an old man of me, Raimi," he yelled after me.

I couldn't contain my laughter as I leapt into my car, putting it into drive. I would find something for tonight, and the party was going to be great.

FOUR HOURS later, I collapsed on my bed, shopping bags splaying out around me comically. It wasn't that I had bought all that much. It just came from different stores that insisted I couldn't consolidate into one bag. I sighed, finishing the last of my coffee before throwing the empty cup into the trashcan. I glanced over at the clock and cursed loudly. Two hours to get ready and I hadn't even showered yet. I was screwed.

I can't stress how quickly those minutes flew by, and in what seemed like the blink of an eye, I stood in front of my mirror, fixing the last details. I couldn't help beaming at my reflection. My hair was straight around my face and hung long down my back. I hadn't held back on my makeup, going for a full-on smoky eye that made my cheekbones so sharp they could cut glass.

I had a crop top on that rode up to show a little peek of skin when I moved around and severely short shorts revealed more than enough long, tan leg, even with black stiletto boots covering my calves. I was touching up the last of my lipstick when the doorbell rang. I grabbed my phone, running down the stairs precariously in the practically stripper worthy heels. Cam was waiting for me impatiently at the door in a bright pink mini skirt and a peasant blouse and bright green heels.

She appraised me quickly, her hair falling silkily in her face. "You look hot. Now let's go," she said, looping her arm through mine and walking me to her convertible with Freddie behind the wheel.

The thing about Cam is that I never knew what she was thinking. Her face and voice had an eerie way of never correlating emotions. Except, of course, when she saw Freddie waiting in the car and grinned broadly at him.

"Get us out of here. It smells like rich kid," Cam yelled.

I rolled my eyes.

"Oh, whatever, Miss Trust Fund," I quipped. They both laughed, and we went to the party like that. Carefree and completely young. I don't think I had ever felt so much like a teenager as in that one moment.

We pulled up in front of an imposing brick colonial unfortunate enough for its adult owners to be away for the weekend. The party was already spilling out onto the front lawn. If the kids putting on this blowout were smart, they'd take it into the backyard before one of the neighbors called the cops.

Freddie handed me the car keys. Even though he'd driven, I gathered that the car was Cam's. She, however, declared me the designated driver. Which was fine with me. They both handed me little slips of paper that described how to get them home from whoever's house we were at. Wow. They'd obviously done this before.

And then the drinking started.

THREE

IT STARTED out with just beer for the majority of kids thronging the house. They must have been waiting until later in the night to get really smashed. But as the party got more and more crowded, some of the more beautiful girls took shots of vodka, chasing it down with Red Bull—to get the taste out, I guess.

Different people had different drinks of choice, I learned soon enough. For Cam, it was rum and Coke, but Freddie went straight for the beer. I was fascinated for a while, just watching everyone interact.

Since I didn't know most of these people, I was able to study them objectively. Most of them struck me as desperate to fit in and desperate to stand out in the crowd. They were actually kind of pathetic as a group. But then, I wanted the exact same things in my heart of hearts. Who was I to pass judgment?

Eventually, I got bored of playing scientist and wandered over to the makeshift bar. It consisted of a long dining room table pulled over in front of a liquor cabinet. The kid manning the bar was mixing everything from gin to Jack Daniels with literally every brand of soda I had ever seen.

Music was thrumming loudly in my ears as I leaned against a wall, taking in everyone that stumbled up to and away from the table. Most of the hard drinkers were girls, interestingly enough. I would've thought it would be the boys getting the girls drunk, but either it was the other way around or the girls were trashing themselves tonight.

It was strange to watch couple after couple sneak away upstairs, in varying degrees of sobriety. Everything was pretty normal, pretty much what I associated with underage drinking and high school parties. For about two hours.

I spied Cam and Freddie weaving through the crowd toward me, arm in arm, both of them smashed as hell. I had to physically catch Cam when they finally reached me in the crush of sweaty bodies. She'd managed to fall off of her high heels as she turned to speak to me.

I smiled carefully down at her. "Hi there, Cam. How ya holding up?" I yelled over the music.

She giggled, taking a big swig of her latest rum and Coke. "I'm great! But Freddie isn't doin' so hot," she slurred, hiccupping.

She swayed as Freddie staggered on cue and grabbed at her arm for balance. He had that whole clammy, faintly gray-green-skin-tone thing going, as if he was going to puke, which wouldn't surprise me with the amount of drinking everyone had been doing. At least neither of them seemed high. Not that I would be able to tell if they were. As a homeschooled kid buried deep in the Bible belt until a couple of months ago, it wasn't like I'd hung out with a whole lot of kids who had access to drugs.

"Cam, do you know where the bathroom is?" I asked.

Despite having no balance and a serious brain-tongue disconnect, she seemed to be otherwise holding her liquor relatively well. She nodded, her eyes going in and out of focus. I was about to take them both to the bathroom and hold Freddie's head while he puked his guts out when I saw something that made me stop.

I took Cam by the shoulders and stared hard at her, forcing her to focus on my carefully spoken words. "Take Freddie to the bathroom. Get him to puke, or at least sit down with him in there for a little bit. I'll meet you over by the bar when you're done. Okay?" I shouted. God, the music just kept getting louder and louder. I had no idea how the cops hadn't been called yet.

Cam nodded as if she'd understood my instructions, and I prayed she would do what I told her to. I knew she would never remember to go back to the bar, but it was worth a shot.

I hurried past her, leaving her staring at me, confused. But I *had* to investigate what I had seen. I weaved my way through the crowd on what passed as the dance floor—I think it was the living room, but all the furniture had been pushed back to the walls. It was a fight to weave my way through more failures to twerk than I had seen in a long time.

I kept my eyes locked on the spot where I'd seen the flash of her long hair, though. I had an overwhelming intuition that this was important. I had walked—well, driven—away against my better judgment once before, and I wasn't about to do it again.

Eventually, the living room bottlenecked into a dining room and then into a kitchen that had previously been all about pristine white marble. Now there were crumbs and spills and smears of barf all over the countertops among the abandoned red plastic cups. I was really starting to dislike alcohol.

When I stepped fully into the kitchen, I caught sight of the drinking game taking place in the breakfast nook. Girl after girl lay down on a wooden table and pulled her shirt up to reveal her belly button. A guy with a bottle of tequila poured a sloppy shot into the girl's belly button, and someone put salt on her neck. Then, whoever wanted would bite a lime, lick her neck, and suck the shot off of her stomach. And finally, the girl would take a shot the guy who had licked her would hand her. I sighed. Complete teenage stupidity, right there.

I was just about to turn around and leave when I spotted Brad across the kitchen, huddled over the kitchen counter with another football player. They looked like they were being secretive about something. Which, of course, made me intensely curious.

I moved closer and dodged around the kitchen island in time to see him pull out a small packet. He tore it open, and a small pill sank to the bottom of a shot glass full of liquid. Three guesses who he was planning to roofie, and the first two didn't count. *Asshole.*

I needed to warn her. But that would mean I had to find her. I stood in the doorway of the kitchen and stood on my tiptoes, but I wasn't tall enough to see over the crowd. There must have been three hundred kids at this damned party.

I turned back to Brad. He would have to lead me to her. He picked up the shot glass and said something to the guy with him. They traded devilish smiles.

He shoved into the crowd of kids in the family room beyond the eating nook, and that was when I saw her. Clare. No way would I be able to muscle through the crowd the way he had. Panic filled me as I watched him offer the drink to her. I tried to shout a warning across the room, but I could barely hear myself. No way would she hear me.

She shook her head no, and my legs almost collapsed in my relief. But then Brad smiled slowly, winding his free hand around her waist. I didn't realize what he was doing until he pushed her forward to lay down on the table. She rolled her eyes but nonetheless lay down and pulled her shirt up.

In disgust, I observed as Brad practically had mouth sex with her bellybutton. Then following with tradition, Clare took the shot that Brad gave her. I swore at myself for my stupidity. I'd forgotten about the shot for the girl afterward.

Clare shuddered as she slammed the shot glass down on the table. Brad tossed the shot glass in the kitchen sink and carried a plastic cup of beer back to her. She took a big drink from it. As for me, I didn't have an attorney for a parent for nothing. I sidled over to the sink and snagged the shot glass. Surreptitiously, I stuffed it in my purse.

I had no idea how long it took for a roofie to take effect. I tried to keep Brad and Clare in sight for the next twenty minutes. Just when I had given up and decided that the pill was probably just sugar to help her get the tequila down, Brad led her to the flying staircase in the middle of the room.

His friends whooped and hollered behind him, catcalling over the blasting electronica being pumped into the room from huge speakers. Clare's eyes were completely glazed over. Her limbs seemed to go limp as she sagged against Brad helplessly. He half carried, half dragged her up the stairs.

I waited for Brad's friends to turn back to their dates and begin grinding again. As soon as they were completely distracted, I sprinted as fast as I could up the stairs. When I got to the top, I looked around frantically. Down the hall, I saw a door just shutting.

Without stopping to think about what I was actually going to do next, I threw open the door. Clare was completely passed out on the bed, her eyes closed and mouth lolling open. Brad rounded on me, anger clear on his face.

"Oh, sorry," I said as casually as I could muster. "Dude, you don't know where the bathroom is, do you? The one downstairs has someone in it, and I've really got to pee," I lied, bouncing up and down for effect.

Brad stalked over to me, herding me back toward the door. "I don't know where the hell the bathroom is, but I know it's not here. So get out," he spat, getting right up in my face.

I frowned. "Brad, buddy, she doesn't look so good," I said, peering around his wide frame.

"That's none of your damn business," he growled. Crap, he was big. And muscular. He looked the same way my dad did when he was drunk enough to get violent at the slightest provocation.

I squared my shoulders, trying to take back a little bit of room from him. "Oh really? Because that looks like a very passed-out girl in some trouble. It would be a shame if someone had seen you slip a pill into her drink about twenty minutes ago and happened to mention that to, I don't know, a cop?" I said, my voice edged in steel.

I took a step forward, trying to force my way past him to get to Clare. He didn't budge. Which I suppose I should have expected. My dad didn't yield an inch when he was drunk, either.

"You have one chance to turn around, walk away, and forget everything you saw. Otherwise, I can make your life a living hell," he said venomously.

I smiled wickedly up at him. "Try me. I witnessed you drugging a girl, and I collected physical evidence of it. I have proof of a serious criminal offense, and all you have is empty threats. There's the door, Brad. Now use it." My voice was strong and steady.

I watched different emotions play over his face, the main one being rage. Neither of us broke eye contact, until finally he pushed past me, slamming the door heavily behind him. I let my shoulders sag, exhaling a breath I hadn't known I was holding.

It struck me forcefully that, although I had a particular talent for getting myself into trouble, I'd really done it this time. I strode over to the bed, trying to rouse Clare. It took several attempts to get her awake. She wiped a hand across her face, disoriented.

I spoke softly but loud enough for her to hear me. "Clare, it's Raimi. Are you okay?"

She blinked up at me blearily. Stupid question, she was definitely not okay.

I racked my brain, trying to figure out a way to tell how severely affected she was as of now. Was this purely the roofie's work, or was the booze partially to blame? "How much have you had to drink, tonight?" I asked.

It took her a minute, but she finally responded. "Raimi? Why do you want to get me drunk?" Her voice was childish, and she rubbed her eyes, smearing her makeup badly. She really was a train wreck right then.

"Just answer my question, Clare. It's important." My voice was urgent in the relatively quiet room. She looked at me quizzically, her big turquoise eyes staring up at me innocently.

"Two shots of tequila, and, umm, three gin and tonics." Her voice was small and slurred.

I swore under my breath. To say she was shitfaced didn't quite cover it. I had to get her out of there. But how? I was nowhere near as strong as Brad, who'd hauled her up there. And after all my hormone shots, I wasn't anywhere near as strong as I used to be, either. For once, I regretted not being a boy.

Well, it wasn't like I had any choice in the matter. It was up to me to get her out of here. I cleared my mind of everything except the task at hand. Carefully, I looped her arm around my neck, already knowing her balance would be next to none. I helped her stand, her body weight

24

hanging heavily against my side. I tried not to grunt in effort as I lifted some of the weight off of her feet. Her head rolled to rest on my shoulder. Her hair tickled my face, spilling down in front of her. She was so weak. So freaking helpless and childlike in this state. Who could do this to any other human being and then rape her?

That was the moment I started to hate Brad.

It was slow, hard work getting her down the stairs, but I did it. Mostly by sheer, stubborn determination not to let that bastard get the best of either of us, and a little bit by coaching Clare when and which foot to step down on.

I thanked my lucky stars when I spotted Cam and Freddie by the bar. Thankfully, they came to me when I waved them over. And when I announced that we were leaving, *now*, they didn't ask any questions. You know a party has gotten really crazy when no one even notices the practically unconscious head cheerleader being led out by a group of junior art nerds. How in the hell could the adults be so unaware of what all their kids were up to these days? Crazy world we lived in.

When we got outside, Cam told me she was pretty sure she'd seen Clare arrive at the party with Brad. And yes, he had a car. God, I hoped he drove it drunk and wrapped it around a tree. Maybe if we were lucky, he'd kill himself in the process.

Freddie was kind enough to help me lay Clare across the backseat. He put her head in his lap so she wouldn't get a concussion on the bumpy way home on top of everything else.

I took out his keys when a frightening thought hit me. My eyes widened. "Cam, do you know where Clare lives?" I squeaked.

Cam stared back at me blankly, not seeming to have a clue.

"What about you, Freddie?" I said hopefully.

He shook his head remorsefully at me in the rearview mirror.

"We both know where she used to live before she got too cool to acknowledge our existence," Cam murmured bitterly.

Crap. Now what? I put the car into drive. I was suddenly very glad I had a good relationship with my parents. Well, good enough for what I had to do next.

I DROPPED off my two inebriated friends at their respective houses. Neither of them seemed concerned about talking their way past their parents. Huh. If I'd shown up at my house that trashed, my mother would've had my head on a platter. I promised Cam I would give her car back to her Monday. She would be passed out tomorrow with a hangover, anyway.

And then there were two. I sighed heavily, turning around to go home while Clare remained unconscious in the backseat. I tried to drive as carefully as I could, but still I heard an occasional groan from the backseat. I winced when we hit a massive pothole just yards from my house.

The scary part was, she didn't even move her head to look and see what had just happened, even though she practically caught air. *Asshole! Asshole! Asshole!* just kept running through my mind. All I could seem to think about were different and colorful ways to describe the depth of Brad's stupidity.

I turned onto my street and pulled to a stop in front of the long walkway to our front door. I put the car in park, taking a deep breath. Even if my parents threw a fit, I owed it to Clare to let her crash someplace safe until morning. I got out of the car, circling around to try to pull her upright.

She complained in incomprehensible mumbles, but I got the gist of her wanting to be left alone. She would freeze to death if I left her in the backseat of Cam's car all night, though.

"We're almost home, Clare, just stay awake for two minutes, okay?" I soothed. "Do what I tell you to, and I promise I'll leave you alone and let you sleep after that."

I was relieved when she nodded her head ever so slightly to indicate she'd heard me and would attempt to cooperate with this exercise of getting her inside. Just like we had at the party, I helped her stay upright. It took some fumbling at the door, but eventually I got my key to catch on the lock. We stumbled through the living room and up the stairs.

I helped her onto my bed, where she collapsed in a heap. I actually had to straighten out her arms and legs for her. God, thinking of what Brad would have done to her in this state made my skin crawl.

I took off her strappy heels. It wouldn't help either of us if she managed to rip my sheets because of her taste in shoes. I turned her on her side so she wouldn't choke to death or suffocate if she puked and propped a pillow behind her to keep her there. Then, carefully, I pulled the blankets up over her.

I think the scariest part of that night was just how helpless she was. It made me shiver. Once she was taken care of, I trudged downstairs, bracing myself to face some serious crap.

I knocked on my parents' bedroom door, the sound of a late-night show on their TV coming faintly from behind it. My mom opened the door, glasses perched on her nose and a book in her hand. I glanced past her. Luckily, my dad was already asleep, most likely after his usual Saturday night bender.

Mom put a finger to her lips when she saw my face and led me into her office down the hall. She closed the door quietly, no doubt trying not to wake my dad up. Not that a marching band would've done the trick once he'd gotten deep into a bottle of scotch.

"What's wrong?" she asked sympathetically. My mom really was a great lawyer. She knew how to get anyone to talk, including me.

I took a deep breath, taking a minute to sort out my thoughts. "Mom, there's a girl in my room upstairs. I'm pretty sure she got drugged at the party, and I was wondering if she could stay here tonight to sleep it off." I added in a rush, not wanting to give her a chance to say no, "I'll sleep in the guest bedroom and drive her home in the morning."

She took a moment to respond, obviously taken off guard. "If she was drugged, then we should get her to a hospital tonight so they can

27

do testing and catch it before the drug leaves her system. Do you know who did it?" Her eyes were piercing, even though they were heavy with lack of sleep.

I should've known she would jump immediately to the legal implications of what I'd said. Suddenly, the shot glass in my purse, still over my shoulder, felt like it weighed a ton. I'd known what had happened was a big deal, but the enormity of my interfering in Brad roofie-ing Clare slammed into me even harder now. Was I willing to make a police statement? To testify against Brad? To drag Clare into the middle of a criminal investigation without her having any say in the matter at all?

Thing was, stuff like this happened to girls all the time. And from what I knew of kids my age, they rarely wanted to drag adults into it, let alone the police. It was stupid to keep their silence and was rooted in even more stupid fears, but it was also the code we teens lived by. If I wanted to be one of them, I had to play by their rules.

I shook my head slowly, decision made. Now to talk my mom down off the legal bridge. "I think there's more going on with her than just being drugged. The guy who did it has something on her. Something he's holding over her. I don't know what it is, but I'm pretty sure she would refuse to take a blood test if she were conscious. Can we just not get involved?"

It felt weird trying to talk my mom out of pursuing one serious situation because a more serious one likely existed. I looked at her pleadingly, silently trying to convince her to stay out of it.

She stared at me long and hard, surprise evident on her face. Her expression passed through skeptical to thoughtful to resigned. "I'm going to trust your judgment on this, Raimi. Do what you need to. But don't hesitate to come to me again if you need help."

And with that, my mom turned around and left me alone in the room. I stared after her for a minute. She was really the best mom ever. I reminded myself to tell her that tomorrow. In the meantime, I'd better check on my impromptu houseguest. I walked back upstairs, suddenly feeling dead tired. Drained.

Clare was still out cold and hadn't moved a muscle. I'd done everything I could for her. I grabbed an old T-shirt and a pair of flannel pajama bottoms and headed down the hall. No guest bedroom had probably ever felt more welcoming to anyone.

LIGHT STREAMED in, slanting with midmorning. I squinted at the open window, disoriented. The minute the events of last night hit me, I sprang out of bed and sprinted to my room. My bed was empty, a yellow sticky note in the center of my pillow. I scanned it quickly.

> *Rain,*
>
> *Your mom told me you brought me home last night. She said you hadn't told her much, and that she wasn't going to ask questions as long as I was all right. Thank you for not getting me blood-tested. Let's keep this between us.—Clare*

With that, I went downstairs, the rest of the day completely normal and uneventful. Except I couldn't get that note out of my mind. Clare didn't even know my name. I had kept her from getting raped. I had let her crash in my house. And she didn't even know my name.

FOUR

I DON'T know what I expected Clare to act like on Monday. But it definitely wasn't how she did act. I walked into Spanish, and she was in her normal seat next to Brad, laughing and talking with her normal friends. She didn't even look up when I walked in.

Stunned, I took my normal chair in the back. I listened to the same old lecture, only on a different verb. I did basically the same worksheet, and everyone left as if nothing had happened over the weekend. I still wasn't even a blip on her radar after everything that had happened. Just another face to walk past in the hall.

I didn't talk to anyone that morning. I didn't even know what I was feeling. But it was a jumble of pretty strong emotions, some of them deeply angry and disillusioned. That was the both good and bad thing about going to a brick-and-mortar school. I didn't have time to think about much of anything except shuffling from one class to the next, and trying to focus on what my teachers were saying through all the background noise of a class full of teenagers.

At lunch, I just sat there toying with my food, not giving anyone the time of day until a girl named Shauna got to dishing about all the hot hookups that had happened at the party.

"So the big news is that Brad slept with Kathy Whittaker. Can you believe that? I mean just look at him! He honestly has the nerve to sit next to Clare like nothing even happened," Shauna declared, her face coiling up in disgust when she looked over at the two of them. She waved a hand dismissively. "I call bullshit on that whole relationship. Serious and total bullshit." Her voice was edged in anger.

I didn't know where it had come from, but at that moment, I loved how truthful sweet, shallow Shauna could be. And then something occurred to me. "Cam, how much do you remember from Saturday night?" I turned to her, urgent.

She looked up at me from her sandwich, deep bags beneath her eyes. It was clear she was still a little shaky from the hangover of a century. "What do you think, genius? Not a thing." Cam shook her head, going back to her lunch.

I turned my attention to Freddie, skewering him with my stare. He sighed. I just glared at him until he blurted a little too innocently, "What?"

I rolled my eyes, pointing an accusing finger at him. "You know something. Start talking, mister." I took my tone of voice right out of my mother's playbook of how to make a witness squirm.

If the other people at the table hadn't been staring at us already, they were now. Freddie shrugged, playing it down as if he didn't know anything. I already had enough bottled up inside me; I didn't need someone I considered a friend to side with the asshole and cover for Brad, too.

"Freddie. Just tell me what you know." My voice was hard, almost emotionless. I had no idea why I felt a need to protect Clare. I didn't owe her anything.

I told myself it was out of pity for her. It was obvious to me that Brad really did have something on her she couldn't afford to let get out. Freddie made no move to say anything until Cam put a hand on his arm and murmured something low enough that only he could hear it.

He nodded at her words, a resigned look on his face, and turned his full attention back to me. "I don't know much, okay? I just remember that Clare was really fucked up, and we took her home. That's all I got." His voice was quiet, only loud enough for our table to hear. Shauna gasped dramatically, and a few of the other kids gave me pointed gazes.

31

I nodded. "Thanks." It was less than I had hoped for, but more than I'd expected. Still, I hated how the teen code was making them all close ranks to protect Brad. *At Clare's expense.* She was the victim in all of this. But everyone seemed determined to make her a victim again by not coming to her defense. Were they all assholes, too, or just scared? Either way, it sucked.

Everyone at the table stared at me, a little bewildered. It was finally Cam who said, "Hang on. You were the only sober person in the entire house, Saturday night. Out of all of us, you should know what happened." Her voice wasn't necessarily accusatory, but it was clear she was suspicious.

The only thing I did in response was nod very slowly, never looking up. And with that, I went back to toying with my food. It wasn't like I was any better than the rest of them at the end of the day.

The table was mostly silent for the rest of lunch.

Afternoon classes were a breeze, and I found myself without homework at the end of the school day. I couldn't help smiling now and then in spite of my foul mood, because hey, life is about the little things. That, and I'm by nature a pretty optimistic person.

I followed my afternoon routine when I got home, grabbing a snack and heading straight upstairs to my room. I went to my computer to check my e-mail before I headed over to YouTube to surf music videos for a while.

I opened the last mail and blinked, startled. That was weird. It was an invitation to join an online chat and instant message service a lot of the kids at school used. I didn't recognize the e-mail address of whoever'd sent me the mail. Intrigued, I clicked the link and downloaded it.

When the little icon popped up, I double-clicked on it, curious. And hey. I had a good antivirus program on this machine. I set up my profile like it told me to and let it load.

In the meantime, I reread Clare's note just like I had been doing for the past two days. I guess I thought if I kept reading it over and over again, I might uncover some sort of hidden message or plea for help.

Or, more likely, I was just crazy. That was definitely a possibility. I jumped when the download completed, and it dinged loudly. It then gave two short beeps. Investigating, I went over to my desk to see what was up.

Apparently, I had two new messages. I didn't know how that was possible, since I'd joined like ten seconds ago, but I didn't question it in that moment like I probably should have.

I clicked on the first one. The profile picture in the top right corner was blank. I read the message quickly, my eyes scanning quickly across my computer screen. What I saw made me want to turn off my monitor and go vomit in the toilet.

You have no proof. She didn't get tested, bitch. Let the games begin.

I clicked on the user info, but it was blank. I didn't need it to know who it was from, though. He had made it pretty clear. But this whole business of how he got to my account before I even made an account was freaking me out. Shaken, I opened the second message without clicking on the profile.

I'm sorry for not staying longer and thanking you in person. Not safe yet. Brad has something on me I can't let him go public with. Stay sane, Rain.

I didn't need to see who it was from, either. There was only one person I knew who called me Rain.

THE NEXT day at school, I kept to myself. I watched the people around me pass by and wondered what it was in their lives that occupied their secret thoughts. Was it as scary as what occupied mine?

I noticed, to my chagrin and fear, that Brad kept shooting glances at me from across the Spanish classroom. I looked away and didn't try to engage him in the middle of class. But in the cafeteria at lunch, I caught him full-on staring at me. This time, I held his gaze, matching him steel for steel. I didn't spend the first sixteen years of my life in

Texas, desperately fighting to be who I was to back down to the first random schmuck who gave me hell.

Shauna saw our staring contest. She whistled obnoxiously. Her beautiful mocha-toned face broke into a bright smile. "Looks like you've got an admirer, Raimi." Her voice was teasing.

I didn't look away from Brad.

Shauna squealed in excitement. "Oh my God. He might be a total ass, but you two would be so cute together!" Her voice was sweet, but the same shallowness I both loved and hated was definitely out in force today.

I chuckled darkly, without humor. "He's not really my type."

IT WAS a small victory, but Asshole was the one to look away first. Okay, so Clare all but draped herself across his lap to force him to look at her, but still. I won round one.

More and more after that, I caught Brad looking at me. Eventually, I learned to just tune him out. He wasn't worth my time at this point. No one knew my secret, and I wasn't going to let him think I had something worth hiding. So life went back to normal.

The week flew by, and I aced all of my tests. Very quickly I was rising to the academic top of my class. Thank you, Mom, for all the great tutoring. Friday came quicker than I thought possible. Oh joy. Another football game to endure.

I was walking out of my last class of the day, Advanced Art, when I saw her in the parking lot. I was surprised she was still here. Almost everyone had already left school since there were no after-school sports on Friday, and the parking lot was basically empty. The only reason I was still here so late was to help with an art assignment Ms. Reynolds had wanted me to set up for the class next week. And a little one-on-one time with a hard teacher was never a bad thing.

Clare was behind the wheel of her car, mascara running down her face. I stood at the edge of the parking lot, not knowing whether I should go to her or not. The wind blew over my face, catching my hair in its crisp chill. The sky was thick with a gray blanket of storm clouds scudding along overhead. I don't know how long I stood there trying to decide what to do.

She wasn't sobbing. There was no shaking. Pain too deep for simple crying emanated from her. The tears just streaked silently down her face, which was more difficult to look at than if she'd been lost in a snot-and-slobber sobfest.

Her hair was a mess, thrown back into a bun that must've taken her under ten seconds. Which was saying something. She was one of those girls who always tried and was always put together. She never came to school in jeans and sloppy hoodies with no makeup and bad hair. Ever. But she looked like hell, right now. Still beautiful. But hell.

Puffy red rims made her eyes stand out so stark and blue that I could see their vibrant color from a good thirty feet away. She just sat there, her knuckles white on her steering wheel, clutching it so hard I thought her nails might draw blood from her palms.

I felt the note in my jeans pocket and thought back to what she had looked like, so helpless, at that party. The eeriest part of seeing her crying now was glimpsing the same resigned self-hatred on her face that I had seen every morning on mine when I looked in the mirror, pretransition.

I felt as if I owed it to her to at least try to find out what was going on. Even if I didn't owe it to her, I did owe it to the fourteen-year-old me who'd decided briefly to kill herself because no one would take the time to talk to her. It had been a close thing for me, staying alive there, for a while.

So, shuffling my books around until I found one of those stupid little plastic packages of tissues my mom insisted on stuffing in my backpack, I strode across the empty parking lot. I got right up to her car's window, and she didn't even notice my presence. I rapped on the thin glass, and it took her a moment to respond, even then.

Eventually, she wiped a hand across her wet face, her hand coming away black with eyeliner and mascara. She rolled down the window a crack. "What?" she croaked.

I stuffed a tissue through the slit in the window. She let it fall into her lap. For the longest time, it sat in her lap, and I honestly thought she was just going to roll up the window, drive away, and never speak to me again. I felt anger roiling off of her like she was building walls of rage to keep people out.

I sighed, leaning against her car. "You know, not everyone is an evil bitch or bastard out to screw you." My voice was tired in the humid air.

She laughed, but it didn't reach her eyes. Clare picked up the tissue and dabbed at her face. Thunder rumbled overhead, ominous and looming. I stood there a moment, waiting for her to respond. She finally put the tissue down, her hands settling restlessly in her lap. Her body seemed to just leak with anxiety, and I desperately wished she would talk to me about it. Eventually, I got tired of waiting for her to talk again.

"I'm one of those lucky individuals who isn't crazy or trying to get something out of you, Clare. Let's be real. There's not much you could tell me that I could pass on. Who would they believe? You can talk to me, if nothing else because, as the new kid, I have a pretty low social ranking around here." I was trying to get her to see that I didn't bite.

She finally turned in her seat to face me, her stare locking on to me with the full force of her turquoise eyes. "What if I told you that I'm a monster?" she asked, dead serious.

I snorted. "Well, then I'd say you're certainly trapped in the body of an angel." The minute that was out of my mouth, I had to restrain my hand from flying to cover my mouth in horror. I prayed I wasn't engaging in some serious blushing, but from the heat in my face, I'd say I was failing.

She laughed, nonetheless. "That's not what I mean." Clare's voice was serious beneath the façade of sardonic amusement.

I nodded sympathetically, trying to summon the right words to help her as best as I possibly could. "Everyone has monsters, demons, they don't want to face. We as teenagers live in hormonal hell right now. And it doesn't help that we're surrounded by a bunch of people living in the same hell, too wrapped up in their own problems to really think about anyone else." I spoke carefully, enunciating my words with precision, not wanting to screw this up.

Clare stared ahead emotionless, her eyes hardening.

I made a noise of irritation. "Don't do that. I can see you putting up walls, right now, as I'm trying to hold a conversation with you and failing to keep your attention."

She did look at me then, like she was trying to figure me out, trying to see the cogs working in my mind, to figure what was causing me to act this way. Finally, she averted her gaze, frustrated.

"Why do you care?" she snapped.

I rolled my eyes. "Oh, get over yourself. Whatever it is can't be that ba—" The window snapped up, cutting me off. I rubbed my forehead. I have to say, guy hormones were a lot easier to deal with. But the effects of estrogen still amazed me.

I raised my voice to be heard through the glass. "That's not what I meant, Clare. Just talk to me, and I promise whatever it is will seem a lot less all-consuming. Sometimes it takes someone from the outside to see what's going on clearly." I rested my hands against her window and peered in at her, tilting my head.

She finally turned her gaze on me, and I saw something in it begging for me to understand. I had to fight the urge to recoil from her intense stare, to actually shy away from the power of it. Not only the power of the raw emotions evident in her eyes, but also in the sheer beauty of it.

I held my breath, waiting for either one of us to do something. An icy raindrop fell onto my head, nestling into my hair. I frowned up at the sky. Fat raindrops began to fall down around me. I heard the soft click of a car door unlocking. Keeping my eyes on the sky, I walked around to the other side of her car and got in. Thunder echoed overhead, filling the air with impatient electricity. I settled into the passenger seat, trying to get comfortable. It smelled like cinnamon and vanilla, spicy with warm undertones.

I put my bag on the floor, and she curled up with her legs on the seat in front of the steering wheel. We watched it rain in silence, and I tried to understand what to do next. Her eyes were unfocused, and she started crying again.

I reached over to her, tentatively placing my hand on her arm. I just brushed my fingertips against her wrist and murmured, "It's okay."

She shut her eyes tightly, crying harder, letting the sobs finally escape.

I covered her hand with mine, and then we just sat there awhile. I held on to her hand tightly as she let the pain flow out.

I knew she would tell me what was going on when she was ready, but right then, she just needed someone to be her rock. Lightning zinged through the sky, and thunder rumbled deeply overhead. But it didn't matter. The only thing that mattered to me right then was that she would be okay, that I would help her be okay even if that meant leaving her alone.

I don't know how long we sat there, but it was a long time. Eventually, her breathing steadied, and her tears started to subside. I smiled calmly at her.

She looked up at me and laughed. "Sorry. I know I look awful when I cry."

I rolled my eyes, snorting. "Oh, whatever. I don't know a girl who doesn't."

She nodded, biting her lip. "Do you ever think it's not worth it?" she inquired softly.

My eyebrows knit together in confusion. "What's not worth it?"

She extricated her hand from mine. I waited a minute before putting my hand back in my lap carefully.

Her breath stammered out, broken. "All of it, everything. Being alive and everything that means." She gestured wildly.

"I think it's worth it," I murmured.

She nodded, looking out the window. "So it's just me, then," she whispered.

I paused a second, deciding if I really wanted to go there with her right then, and how much to tell her. But if I expected her to tell me what was wrong, then I probably would have to reveal something as well. There's always a certain give and take when you deal with people. Which is why I don't usually *deal with people.*

"I didn't used to, though," I said quietly. "I was pretty convinced everyone was out to screw me for the longest time. And I was right to a degree. I spent a long time shutting everyone out, not telling anyone what was going on inside my head. It got bad for a while, and it just kept getting worse until I told my parents, and they were able to step in and help. But I was alone for what seemed like an eternity, just waiting for someone to see the hell I was in."

I could barely hear my own voice over the rain, which was pelting down outside harder than ever. I thought that maybe my words had gotten lost in the volume of the storm. Part of me hoped they had. It was hard for me to go back to that place in my mind, even if it was only a memory now.

"How did you fix things?" Clare's head rested against the window, and I could see the reflection of her lips moving on the glass.

"I didn't. The people around me helped me find myself again, I guess. It was hard at first, but now it's the easiest thing in the world to wake up and be happy. I highly recommend it," I teased.

Clare smiled blankly against the glass. "You make it seem so simple."

I chuckled, pulling my legs up into a ball like she had. "It's not simple at all. It sucked for a while. Took me forever to realize it's not all about the people I was surrounded by. And with that realization came the one that it's not all about me, either."

She nodded, exhaling heavily. "Anyways. Thanks for sitting with me. Can I drop you off somewhere?"

I knew that this conversation was over. In a way, it was a relief because it meant there was no more threat today of letting someone see my secrets. But in the back of my mind, I also knew it meant I wouldn't get to see hers today, either.

"No, it's okay, my car is right over there. And don't apologize. Don't ever apologize for being you."

I let myself out quietly, walking into the downpour. I have to say, in that moment, the rain had never felt so good.

CLARE WATCHED as Rain walked away, her hair clinging to her body, her clothes slick and dark with water. She didn't want to admit it to herself, but as Rain walked away, it was hard to deny that thing she'd been denying forever.

"Good-bye, Rain." Her whisper echoed around her in the small confines of her car. Maybe Brad wasn't the end of the world. Maybe life could be better. Maybe she could be free.

FIVE

LATE THAT night, I got a rather frantic call from Cam. "Oh my God, you have to get over here right now!"

"Why? What's wrong? Are you okay?" I grabbed my car keys, not caring I was in sweatpants and a baggy T-shirt with my hair up in a messy bun.

"I'm fine, I'm fine. You just have to come over this instant!" Cam wailed.

I jammed my feet into the nearest pair of shoes, rushing out the door into the humid night. "Okay, I'll be there in three minutes." I jumped into my car, putting it in reverse. I think I broke every speed limit I encountered on my way over, but it was for a good cause. When I got to Cam's house, I took the steps to her front door two at a time.

Panting, I pounded on her door. "Cam! I'm here Cam!"

She opened the door leisurely, resembling my dress for comfort. She smiled slyly. "Hey, babe. Come on in, the movie is just about to start," she drawled.

I frowned, confused. She didn't appear to have any life-threatening injuries, and there were no signs anyone had broken in. "Wait. So you called me over here, scared the crap out of me, and you just want to watch movies?" I asked in disbelief.

Her face broke into an even bigger smile as Freddie called, "And to eat popcorn! Don't forget the popcorn!" His big goofy grin deflated any anger I might have had as he came to the door.

I let a huge smile sweep across my face. "You guys suck."

THROUGH SEVERAL bowls of popcorn and two *Saw* movies, we all just sat together on Cam's couch. I hadn't realized my secret love of scary movies until that night. I was relaxed, just sitting there with them, being a teenager. As Cam bounded into the kitchen to start yet another bag of popcorn in the microwave, I felt a pang of guilt deep in my stomach. They had no idea about my past. Of course, I had only known them for a sum total of two weeks. But still, they were the closest things I had ever had to real friends. At least after the transition.

I sighed heavily, picking at the wool blanket we were all sharing. I had just opened my mouth to say something, anything, to them about my past when my phone buzzed. I stared at the screen.

Gotchya. Your secret is mine, fag. She told me about the car.

I couldn't believe it. What had Clare told him? I hadn't said anything about my secret, just that I knew what it was like to be lost. It didn't make any sense!

Freddie was finally the one to poke me out of my haze. "Did you hear any of what I just said?" he teased.

I stared at him, my eyes wide with fear.

He scowled. "What?"

I fidgeted, my eyes flicking back and forth between him and my phone. I couldn't say anything, my mouth just hung open. Cam screamed from the kitchen. It was somewhere between rage, surprise, and happiness.

"Oh my God, Clare and Brad finally broke up! Oh! My! God!" Cam's voice echoed loudly from the kitchen. Freddie and I both took a moment to absorb that in the other room when Cam's shrill scream sounded again.

"Clare's a lesbian!"

It hit me like a ton of bricks. The breath was physically knocked out of my lungs. I couldn't breathe. I seriously couldn't draw a molecule of air into my lungs. That was what Brad had on her. The son of a bitch just shoved her out of the closet like a rag doll because she didn't want to be raped by him anymore. It all made sense now.

I sat in shocked silence while Cam showed Freddie something on her phone. She hustled over to me once she had shown him. He was covering his mouth in disbelief. Cam placed the phone right in front of my face. There was no denying it. Someone had posted a picture of Clare and a tall redhead I didn't recognize making out. They had their hands up each other's shirts, so it couldn't be equated to an innocent little kiss after they had too much to drink.

I shook my head slowly. "So this was the blackmail material Brad had on her."

Cam and Freddie both shot me quick glances. "What makes you think that?" Cam snapped.

I shrugged. "Doesn't it seem just a little suspicious to you that at the exact same time he and Clare break up, someone anonymously posts that picture?" I knew I was right. And I reeled in disbelief that someone was capable of that type of cruel, calculated blackmail.

Freddie nodded. "It makes sense. Everyone thought he had something on her. But none of us thought it was this…." His voice trailed off, his eyes unfocusing.

Cam snorted. "That's because it's sick. I can see why she would do anything to keep something like that hidden," Her voice was literally toxic. It dripped with venom.

I leaped to my feet, anger boiling in my stomach. It was people like Cam, saying things like that, who had driven me to want to die. I literally shook from the fire coursing in my veins.

"How in the hell can you say something like that? How is loving someone wrong? So what if she likes girls? Why is that a problem, Cam?" I shouted.

Cam's eyes widened in surprise at my angry outburst. Freddie jumped up in between us, trying to shield Cam from me, if I had to guess.

"Whoa, whoa, whoa. That's not what Cam is saying," Freddie said reasonably.

I didn't care at that point, though. I was so furious I could spit.

It took a minute for Cam to recover. She twisted her face up into an ugly sneer.

"And who made you so high and mighty? Talk like that to enough people, and they'll start to think you're some filthy dyke," she spat.

I inhaled sharply.

Even Freddie was aghast at her. "Cam, what in the actual hell is going on with you? I've never seen you like this." He spoke low, his voice breathy with shock.

I shook my head. "You ignorant, judgmental bitch. Do you have any idea what it's like to wake up every morning and hate yourself? Because I bet that's what it's like for Clare. You and everyone else in this whole school have watched Brad practically rape her the minute he didn't think someone was watching for the past two years. Can you even wrap your tiny mind around how terrified she must have been of being outed to have stayed with him?"

Freddie's eyes widened in horror. "Oh my God. That poor girl," he whispered. Cam just laughed. "She should be afraid. Being gay is *wrong*, Raimi. It's a sin." It looked as if Freddie was going to pass out, and as if Cam was willing to jump over his about-to-be-prone body to strangle me.

I laughed so hard I couldn't breathe. Not that it had the slightest thing to do with humor. "Oh my God. You're hilarious, Cam. It's so cute to watch you be all Christian after I watched you get so wasted you could barely stand. I applaud you for your fake devout faith. I hope you know that people like you are the reason kids kill themselves. You should be proud of yourself, really."

With that, I grabbed my coat and walked out. I was extremely glad I hadn't told them anything. She was just like every other close-minded, hateful homophobe I had ever met. And Freddie wasn't much better for standing there and letting her say all of those horrible things.

At least he'd had the decency to feel a morsel of sympathy for what Clare had been through.

Oh, well. They wouldn't be missed.

WHEN I stormed into my house, my mom didn't ask questions. She just folded me into a huge hug. Whether I wanted to admit it or not, I had trusted Cam and Freddie to be decent human beings. And what was worse was that, as scared as I was for Clare, I was more terrified of what Brad had on me. The most horrible part of it was not knowing. I wanted so desperately to tell my mom as her arms encircled me, a spoon still in her mouth.

But she was a lawyer, and the minute she got wind of any of this, she would go all legal on me and call in her best lawyer friends, and it would be a complete mess. No, I couldn't talk to her.

I might've gone to my dad if he hadn't been so uptight about the whole trans thing in the first place. Not to mention he was also probably out with one of his business consultants. Or finding peace at the bottom of a bottle.

Luckily, my mom seemed to understand why I usually didn't tell her things. She held me back at arm's length and looked deeply into my eyes. "I love you. No matter what, sweetheart. Now let me make you some cocoa."

THREE CUPS of hot chocolate with my mom later, I trudged up the stairs dejectedly. I pulled out my phone. I found the picture of Clare—not that it was hard to find. Everyone in the damned school was sending it to everyone they knew—and took a screenshot of it.

It's not that I liked looking at it. It was a reminder to me of the kind of person Brad was, and that kept me moving. It kept me from just sitting down and letting the anger, the fear, and the emptiness seep in.

Once in my room, I sat down heavily at my desk. Before I knew what I was doing, my fingers were flying across my keyboard, pulling up a screen that I didn't want to see. I closed my eyes, my fingers continuing to move.

I don't know what or who you're talking about. Is there any chance you have a wrong e-mail address or something in your contact information?

My finger hovered over my mouse. I clicked send. Then, going to my other instant message window, I saw that she wasn't online. Hastily, I shut off my computer. I assured myself that she wouldn't see anything I sent her anyway. I'd been in her shoes before, and I knew without a doubt that the first thing she would do is turn off or throw out every device over which anyone could take potshots at her.

In other words, I made up a simple excuse for a complex reason why I didn't IM Clare. It wasn't my fault that she had finally gotten rid of Brad. *Right?* And it was a great thing that she had gotten out from under his blackmailing, cruel thumb.

But I couldn't help but wonder. Was she ready to be out of the closet? Or was she just running from the psychologically bloodstained bars Brad had caged her behind? Either way, it was out of my hands now.

I ran my palms over my hair, shivering. Memories of Texas, of getting beat up behind the bleachers day after day, the anonymous posts detailing when, where, and how I should kill myself, all raced through my mind.

I closed my eyes and wanted to scream. God, it was all coming back. The bone-cracking fear of walking down the hallways every day and knowing that everyone who saw you was not only judging you but condemning you as less than human. Less than human. Less than human. Demon. Devil. Sinner.

I cried silently, trying to push back the hell I had escaped, and only barely with my life.

There was another reason that I hadn't sent an IM of support to Clare. I was too terrified for myself to be terrified for her.

SIX

I HELD my books close to my chest as I hurried through the halls Monday morning, keeping my head down. I didn't glance up, desperately hoping I wouldn't be noticed and just as desperately fearing my hope would not be realized. I practically sprinted into Spanish, flinching before I even hit the doorway.

Except, where I was expecting laughter and derision pointed my way, no one even gave me a second look. Frowning, I took my usual seat in the back and watched the social dynamic going on in front of me. Brad was the center of everyone's attention.

Maybe, just maybe, I wasn't outed.

I couldn't help but sigh in relief, sagging against the back of my chair. I then immediately strained forward to try to catch some snippets of conversation.

"Dude… I mean did you ever know?" That was from Chase, one of Brad's closest friends.

"Nah, it was a total surprise. I mean, she had always been pretty kinky in bed, but I had no idea it was because she wanted a chick to do all that stuff to her. It's screwed up, man, it's screwed up," Brad muttered.

Chase thumped him on the back. "That sucks, dude. Doesn't it freak you out that you guys dated for so long?"

Brad shook his head and laughed darkly. "Let's just say this. She may be gay… but she knows her way around the bedroom." Then the asshole pulled out his phone and showed it to his fellow asshole. "Look at that. Mmm hmm. Nah, I don't regret tapping that." He scrolled through what I was just going to go ahead and assume were naked pictures that he himself had made her take.

The more I thought about it, the more I could see her pleading with him to stop and not make her do these things. Yup, and then he would pull out his phone, wave the picture of her and the redhead under her nose, and she would choke down her tears and do whatever he said.

She was his living blow-up doll, a toy he had complete control over. It was *sick*. It honestly was a miracle that the AP Spanish class didn't witness its first homicide, then and there.

My terror of Brad knowing I was a lesbian, too, breezed right out of my mind as I was taken over by sheer rage. I had spent too long being treated like a subhuman substance, random goo someone had stepped in and ruined their shoes on, to do nothing about him using her as a sex toy whenever and however he wanted. I was just about to get out of my chair and smash his phone on the floor when she walked in.

It was the worst I had ever seen her look, which was still pretty good. Annoyingly beautiful, in fact. Her hair was pulled back into a familiar I-don't-feel-like-trying-today bun, her eyes puffy and red from crying. She had no makeup on and was in jeans and a severely oversized sweatshirt. Her shoulders were hunched, and she held her books a lot like I had.

Everyone's stares shot to her and never left her, scrutinizing her. Her face looked gaunt, like she hadn't eaten or slept in two days. Which made a lot of sense.

She walked past her normal seat in front of the Beast, her eyes staying on the ground.

No one said a word. Instead, they did exactly what they knew how to do best. They judged and condemned her as something nonhuman. I could see the look in each and every one of their eyes. I felt sick. Then she looked up, her piercing blue eyes going straight to my face.

I met her gaze for a moment. *And then I looked down at my desk.*

She stopped abruptly in her path. Looking stunned, she just stood there for a moment. She slid into the nearest empty seat a few rows in front of me.

Clare had just asked permission to seek haven with me. She just wanted to sit with me so that she wouldn't have to face the wrath all of her classmates would bring down on her alone.

But I had told her no.

I had not recognized her as a goddamn human who was capable of sitting with me like a normal person.

I balled my fists up, anger swelling back up in me. Except what I told myself was anger was really fear. Not only had I stooped in that moment to the lowest level of the people around me, but I had also just locked the closet door on myself.

I was now officially closeted. And not only had I turned my back on someone in terrible pain, who I knew was struggling, but I had turned my back on someone who was going through exactly what I had two and a half years ago.

The bell rang for class to start. Our teacher was running late and hadn't arrived yet.

I stood carefully, packing my things one by one with extreme care. I set my mouth in a grim line, and without a second glance back, I walked out of that classroom.

I was despicable. And I wasn't about to let Clare see me continue to be exactly like the people she was surrounded by.

I went out to my car, unlocking the doors and taking time to start the engine before I began shaking. I drove home as carefully and safely as I could, even though I couldn't see through the bleary tears flowing from my eyes.

LIFE IS just one big game of picking sides. Actually, no. It's really just one long string of consecutive decisions we're forced to make, or that we make on our own. And then, from the decisions we make, we're sorted onto the side we play for. Kind of like Harry Potter. Except there's no good house, no house that's a compilation of bad eggs. We're all just flawed people making decisions as best as we can. We're not good or bad. We're just human.

If we really want to try to measure good versus bad decisions, then we have to understand that it varies from person to person. Point of view is crucial in trying to grasp why people act like they do.

For instance, maybe Brad had an unsatisfying home life; therefore, he sought pleasure from sex in the most twisted ways to sate some deep-rooted desire for love. Or maybe I was smoking crack, and he was just a colossal douchebag.

Either way, Brad had already made a long series of decisions that had landed him here. As had I, as had Clare. As did every single human being on the earth.

I had to smile sadly to myself, sick to my stomach. We are all such masochists and sadists sometimes, without even realizing it. I had a big decision to make. It would definitely change which side I had been assigned to so far at school.

If nothing else, it would have a direct effect on someone else. And those decisions are always the scariest.

I thought through the possibilities in my head, playing out different scenarios. There was always the obvious option of talking it over with an adult or authority figure. Except all the fake support they would lend would be bullshit.

Parents and administrators weren't the ones who stopped fights from happening or blocked vicious Internet posts, or would stop the general torment that would inundate Clare if the school went ahead and acted like I thought it would.

I sighed heavily. If I knew more about Clare's parents, maybe I could get a better handle on her situation at home and how much support she could expect from that direction. A big part of being scared and in the closet was being afraid of how your parents would react. I knew.

Of course, I was a complete hypocrite for wanting her to come out to her family. God knew I hadn't done it with mine in the healthiest or safest way. My parents found out I was gay in the suicide note beside my bed when they found me passed out with a bunch of empty pills bottles around me.

I sighed. So that option for getting Clare some help was probably out. I thought through a few more possibilities, but I had absolutely no idea how to help her that didn't involve myself directly.

Well. Crap.

I could lie to myself and say that I didn't want to help, that this wasn't something I had intentionally taken on. So then why did I go to her in her car on Friday? It would have been perfectly acceptable and extremely easy to have just walked past her car and not given it a second thought. I'd had nothing to do with what had happened to her. Right?

But whether I want to admit it or not, I felt like I owed her. Besides, I wanted to help her. Something about her, how she'd just sat there and cried like it was normal, had compelled me to help her in the first place.

Maybe a little part of me had wanted to help fix her and, in doing so, put the pieces of her back together in a puzzle shaped to fit my liking. It was sick to say, but it was true. We all have delusional, screwed up ideas of what other human beings are meant to be. And if we meet someone who isn't quite like our ideal image of them but is still malleable, then why wouldn't we try to reform him or her into exactly what we want?

We all have a little Brad in us. For better or worse and in different amounts, but either way, the drive to make other people our own, just how we want them to be, is still there. Anyone who says they don't ever have that impulse is lying to themselves.

My mind wandered to all of the ways I could help her, all the ways to worm myself into her life, so I could be there to help her superglue the parts of herself back together. At the end of the day, shaping someone and helping them become a new person isn't all bad.

51

If Brad had used his influence over her in a positive way, maybe he actually could have helped her become a better person.

But this wasn't about Brad. This was about Clare and trying to figure out what to do to help. Problem was, the only way to help someone was to actually *help* him or her.

I groaned, rolling onto my stomach on my bed. It was frustrating how something so seemingly simple could be so complicated that the ramifications were mind-boggling. I sighed.

The thought of being a friend to Clare and being subjected to the ridicule and suspicion of everyone at the school wasn't nearly as scary as the thought of being consumed in the feelings I had experienced in class when I turned my back on her.

At the end of the day, it all boiled down to whether or not I could live with myself if I chose the latter.

Yep, life was going to suck for a while, maybe even a long time. But it would get better. It had to.

SEVEN

WHEN I got to school on Tuesday, I was ready to stand ardently by Clare's side. She and I could take on the world together if she could forgive me for turning away and let me help her.

But she didn't show for Spanish class. She wasn't anywhere to be seen at school, and the gossip at lunch was that she was too humiliated to show her face. Confused, I went through my day in outward normalcy. Had I blown my one chance to do the right thing for her?

Cam and Freddie surprised me at lunch by apologizing. Cam said she hadn't known what she was saying or stopped to think about what any of it had meant. Her explanation echoed all through my head that night as I reviewed my science notes.

"I didn't really understand what I was saying, Raimi. I mean, God. When Clare walked into the lunchroom Monday, it was like she had the plague or something. Everyone just looked down, and anyone who did look at her said the most awful things. It was horrible. I realized they sounded like I had on Sunday. I was ashamed, just sitting there, watching it."

Cam had one thing right. Sometimes the worst crime of all was inaction.

Wednesday morning, I was ready for Clare to walk through those doors. I would help her, and we could take on the stares together. And then she didn't show. Again.

I sat with Cam and Freddie like usual and asked them if they would be okay with Clare sitting with us once she was back. They shared a long-suffering look and eventually nodded reluctantly at me. Shauna agreed readily enough, too.

I couldn't get an answer out of any of the other kids who usually sat at our table. I honestly thought that some of them would leave if she sat with us. That was okay. A few empty seats would just mean more room for our stuff during lunch.

Thursday morning, I was sure Clare would show. I was positive that this would be the day that I would get to show my support to her, to the school, and most importantly, to myself. I needed to make a difference with her, to distinguish myself from the backdrop of mindless sheep that just accepted people making her life a living hell. I had to prove that I would be there for her.

And yet, the day passed by utterly Clare-less. It was getting stifling to walk through these halls and wonder what she was doing, if she was okay, if she was angry with me, or if she was too busy dealing with her pain to be angry at anyone.

Friday, I warily awaited a no-show from Clare. There was a party Saturday night that everyone was talking about. It was supposedly going to be so wild that even Shauna was wary of going. I loved Shauna, but she was crazy when it came to partying. I begged off of going, telling the group hastily that I was busy. Everyone else at the table had an excuse not to go either, mumbling about various classes and tests they really needed to crack down and study for.

We all pretended to believe each other out of courtesy. But at the end of the day, it was because none of us had a particular interest in going to jail for one party.

LATE SATURDAY night, a loud banging at my front door startled me awake. I regained consciousness slowly. I had been sleeping on the couch in the family room, having passed out while trying to read some mind-numbing tome for my English class.

I rubbed my eyes, confused. Neither of my parents were home. They had taken Zach on a fishing trip somewhere across the state. The noise outside didn't subside as I crept into the kitchen warily. The clock read 1:06 in the morning. Grabbing the biggest knife I could find, I proceeded to the front door.

Breathing heavily with the heat of adrenaline coursing through my veins, I threw open the door with the knife outstretched as a warning. Clare blinked blearily at me through a stained face full of tears. One of her eyes was swelling, developing what looked like a really painful bruise.

I started to lower the knife to my side and opened my mouth to speak, but she leapt forward and enveloped me in a hug. I reached up to hold her back, but the knife slid into her stomach like butter. Her eyes widened in horror and pain as she recoiled away from me. I screamed in fear when her body sank to the floor.

I held her head in my hands, shrieking for her to stay alive. Her eyelids closed in resignation, her turquoise pupils dilated. Clare's breath stopped entirely. She was dead, and I had killed her.

My eyes shot open.

I was on the couch.

Breathing heavily.

My clothes stuck to me with the same cold sweat clinging to my forehead.

It was just a dream.

Ohmigod. Only a dream.

A freaking nightmare.

But on a small scale, it was exactly what I had done to her on Monday. I didn't go back to sleep that night. The only thing I really knew at that point was that I had to see her and try to fix things if they were broken. Which they were.

SUNDAY MORNING, I left the house in jeans and a comfortable sweater. The air had taken a sudden turn toward frigid. Well, it was cold to me, at least, a recently transplanted southerner. I was on my way to the coffee shop a few blocks from our house, humming along to the radio, when a text dinged on my phone. I didn't think anything of it. I was one of the very few responsible teenage drivers who didn't text and drive.

The coffee shop was mostly deserted except for a few people reading the paper in the farthest corners from the entrance. I ordered a double-shot latte, already starting to feel the effect of not sleeping after that god-awful dream last night.

Taking a sip of my steaming drink, I sat down at one of the quaint oak tables. I was just finishing writing my report for Lit (not sleeping is, however, good for finishing boring required reading) when the door gusted open, letting in a rush of freezing air. I shivered in my sweater when I looked up.

Clare stared at me like a deer in the headlights. Her big blue eyes looked even bigger and bluer in the gray early morning light filtering through a heavy haze of clouds.

I stared at her for a minute, not quite believing it was her. Belatedly, I started to stand up just as she turned to leave. Thankfully, she stopped when I hastily pulled out the chair across from me and sat back down in mine. I stretched my hand out, motioning for her to take a seat. She stared at me for a minute before closing the door behind her and taking a single, tentative step toward me.

I smiled and stood up again, walking over to her. She rubbed her hands uneasily across her jeans, smiling hesitantly.

"Let me buy you a coffee," I said.

She just nodded. It was the least confident I had ever seen her. She bordered on being downright skittish. She didn't speak because the barista already knew what her "usual" was. She didn't speak when she sat down across from me, either.

She sipped at her hazelnut-scented coffee and grimaced at the first sip. I raised a questioning eyebrow at her. "Wrong drink?" I murmured.

Clare laughed a little. "I hate coffee, but I love caffeine. So I get a triple shot of espresso with as many pumps of hazelnut and vanilla syrup as they're allowed to put in one drink."

God, that sounded disgusting. I opened my mouth, and then closed it, making her laugh even harder.

I shook my head, shrugging as I leaned back in my seat to study her. "I never took you for a caffeine addict."

She snorted. "I'm not an addict. I can stop any time I want."

I rolled my eyes. "Yeah, I'm sure you'll quit right after the world ends."

A blush colored her face—which was a definite improvement over the vampirically pale look she'd been working when she came in here. She looked out the window, toying with the strings on her black-and-orange hoodie. I sighed. It had obviously been Brad's.

Her hair was loose and wavy, for once not curled or straightened into submission. And she wasn't wearing a stitch of makeup. I had to say, it was the most real she had ever looked to me. It wasn't as if she was this perfect, unattainable Barbie doll anymore.

I tilted my head. "If you don't mind my asking, why are you still wearing his hoodie?"

She didn't look at me. Instead, she murmured quietly, "I do mind."

I nodded, assuming it was still a little too fresh for her. Mentally, though, I sighed. The twisted psychology of clinging to her abuser's clothes was beyond my limited understanding of such things.

"So what's going on in your life, Rain?" she asked quietly. "You already know what's going on in mine."

I chuckled softly. "You know my name isn't Rain, right?" I looked up from my cup to her face.

She was staring intensely at me, her blue eyes vividly alive on my face. "I know." She didn't say anything more.

I sighed, not understanding why she was so difficult to decipher sometimes. "I'm fine. Passing all of my classes, so that's good," I murmured.

Clare just continued to look at me. I felt as if she was expecting me to continue, so I did. "Everything is going great. My parents and I are good, my friends and I fought, but we're good now. Really, everything is pretty mundane in my little corner of the world," I said.

Her gaze kept on holding mine. "Why did you fight?" she inquired.

I tapped my fingers against the wooden table. "You," I responded.

Clare looked away as an ashamed pang crossed her face. "Well, that's no good," she whispered.

Outside, a patter of rain fell hard and heavy all of a sudden. How appropriate. I took a moment to gather my thoughts.

Then, I admired the ceiling as I commenced talking. I really didn't want to have to see her reaction when I muttered, "My friends had a pretty harsh reaction when they first saw the picture. I more or less told them to get their heads out of their asses, and that they had no idea what they were saying."

I chickened out on peeking at Clare as I continued. "Cam returned the favor by throwing the Bible in my face, which is utter crap by the way, considering she is anything but Christian. Anyway, I just wasn't going to stand there and let them trash you because I know how hard it can be," I finished in a rush. I kept staring at the ceiling. Fascinating stuff, ceiling tile.

She cleared her throat, but I kept my gaze fixed on one tile in particular. "Rain," she said.

"Yeah?" My voice was quiet.

She paused.

I heard one of the customers leave, the sound of rain filling the small space loudly until the door closed again, muffling the storm.

Clare obviously had no idea what to say next.

I finally looked down at her, letting a big gust of air out of my lungs. Her eyebrows were knitted together in concentration. I guess it was her turn not to meet my eyes because she was doing a thorough examination of the floor.

"What do you mean, you know how hard it can be?" she mumbled low. "Have you… been through something like this before?"

My breath caught. My phone dinged again from my bag. I ignored it. "I meant exactly what I said," I replied.

She didn't breathe for a minute, and I was reminded of my terrible dream. Her eyes danced across my face, alight. Her perfect teeth were bright in the shaded room.

"Rain, are you gay?" She asked it with so much awe that I had to giggle a little.

I shook my head and said patiently, "Yes, Clare, I'm a lesbian."

And not two seconds later, Brad and a group of his friends walked in. Clare paled considerably, her shoulders freezing with tension. I didn't say a word as they all shot us poisonous glares, Brad's the most terrifying and worst of them all. He pointed at Clare and laughed a little, meanly.

She recoiled like he had hit her. I reached across the table and seized her hand in mine. Her eyes got huge, and she tried to pull back as she looked back and forth between me and the boys. I squeezed her hand, not moving a finger.

We were in this together, whether she liked it or not. One of the boys, no doubt thinking himself very clever, whistled at us. But I had caught her terrified stare with mine, and I wasn't about to let her look away.

Eventually, an eternity later, she returned my squeeze, as a tiny hint of a smile spread across her features. The boys didn't seem to know what to do with us, and they eventually left. But not before my phone dinged a third time.

Clare flicked her gaze to my bag. "Are you going to get that?"

I had a hunch that it was a certain psychopath IM'ing me anonymously. And frankly, as I watched Brad walk out of the shop and into the downpour, I didn't care if people knew or not. But that could've been the lack of sleep talking.

Either way, though, I was making this decision right here, right now, with Clare as my witness.

"Absolutely not."

EIGHT

I EVENTUALLY pulled my hand away from Clare's and checked my phone. The only incoming message was from the app Brad's earlier messages had come through on. Without hesitation, I deleted it.

Clare and I talked for what seemed like hours in that coffee shop, going through three more caffeinated beverages each. I wasn't going to sleep till about Wednesday. When we looked out the window, it was still pouring, but the sky was dark and threatening now, through the rain.

I glanced over at her and was rewarded with an absolutely beaming smile. She was happy, and that's all the confirmation I needed that I wasn't a nuisance to her. She was actually enjoying herself. And hey, if I gave her a tiny reprieve from the misery everyone else was busy heaping on her head, then it was a day well spent.

When the sun started to set, the gray clouds growing ever grayer, I sighed in regret. "Well, I guess this is it for tonight. School is going to come really early tomorrow, considering I'll be up all night after all that caffeine."

Clare cocked her head at me, an eyebrow rising in amusement. "You were actually planning on going tomorrow?"

"I mean, it is school… so you kinda have to go," I mumbled.

She laughed freely, attracting the attention of the other people in the shop. But then, she was just that kind of girl. "Oh, c'mon, Rain. A little hooky never hurt anyone."

She winked mischievously, then added, "You're such a goodie-two-shoes! School will be closed tomorrow, anyway. Do you not see the major ice storm brewing outside?"

She flicked her fingers casually at the window and motioned for me to sit back down. I did so, shaking my head. Of course, I couldn't tell when a winter storm was coming. I'd never seen one before.

Clare leaned forward, a devilish smile playing over her full lips. "I'll let you in on a little secret. Weather always has a way of turning bad when I need it to. And right now, I feel some major winter badness brewing up in the sky. I'll bet you anything it sleets for an hour or two this evening and then turns into the ice storm of the century. School will definitely be closed tomorrow... and Tuesday also."

The way she spoke quietly, just for my ears, it was like she and I were the only people in the world. Tension crackled into the air between us, charged with something. But I didn't know what.

I cleared my throat, and said a little more huskily than I would've liked, "What would you like to bet on that?"

She closed her eyes and hummed a short, sweet note to herself. Yep, there was definitely something in the air. If it wasn't crack cocaine, it was something equally heady and addictive.

"How about dinner and a movie? My treat?" The moment the words were out of her mouth, she blanched paper white.

I leaned back as the tension snapped in two and broke abruptly. She didn't say anything. Her eyes stared at something I couldn't see, as if she was reliving a long ago memory.

I frowned. "Clare? Are you okay?"

Eventually, she shook her head like she was knocking cobwebs away. "Yeah. I'm fine." But she didn't sound fine. And she didn't say another word.

My brow creased in worry. "Hey, forget about dinner and everything." I prayed my voice wouldn't betray the pang of disappointment I felt in my gut.

She shook her head again. "No, no, it's good. I'll call you." She was in a hurry all of a sudden to stand up and gather her things.

I picked up my laptop and shoved it in my bag. She turned in a rush toward the door and stopped suddenly. Into that frozen moment, I heard the sound of something harder than water splatting onto the asphalt outside. Son of a gun. Sleet.

I tilted my head a little to study Clare quizzically. I swear, she looked like she'd seen a ghost. "Umm, Clare, I don't think you have my phone number."

"Oh," she murmured, as the spell that had held her transfixed broke. But her eyes were still fixated on something outside the coffee shop or maybe something inside her mind.

Slowly, her head turned in my direction. A wooden smile plastered itself onto her face. "Let me get that from you, then." Her voice was hollow.

I took a step toward her and touched her forearm gingerly. "Clare. What's wrong?"

The smile slipped off of her face like an echo bouncing off her soul, fleeing farther and farther from her. "Nothing's wrong," she mumbled.

She was lying.

I snorted and promptly dragged her back down to sit with me. I clutched her forearm, begging with my eyes for her to confide in me. "Is it Brad? I swear to God, he's not going to do anything else to you. So help me—"

She cut me off. "It's not Brad. Not exactly." Her eyes were like glass and gave away absolutely nothing.

"Tell me," I pleaded.

She flinched almost as if I had slapped her. "No. It's not… it's not something I can talk about. Not yet. Please, just respect that and drop it."

It dawned on me that I would never ever be able to push her for things. She had spent almost three years being knocked around by

Brad. Who knew what kinds of things he had forced on her. I could never be like him, not to her. She deserved that, at least. I withdrew my hand from her arm immediately.

"Of course, I respect that. I'll back down. Sorry for intruding," I said formally.

She blew a piece of hair out of her face impatiently, her eyes finally deglazing a little. A smile flickered ironically on her lips as she murmured, "I said drop the subject, not me."

I breathed a sigh of relief. She was back to her usual playful self. Although, she was definitely still distracted. Something unpleasant was definitely lurking in her mind, but she seemed to have come mostly back to the present.

She squared her shoulders and pulled my hand back onto her forearm. Her expression was the epitome of smugness when she said. "So, about dinner tomorrow night, since I am never wrong about the weather."

I glanced outside, and sure enough, silvery ribbons of sleet were falling more thickly now.

She continued, "There's this great little Italian restaurant a couple of blocks from the movie theater. And because I'm a brat and I've seen way too many cheesy pictures online, we're going to walk through the snow to see the movie. Oh, and just so you're aware, I'll be at your house at around ten o'clock tomorrow morning to bring you back here for a coffee. And then we're going to a pizza parlor down the street for lunch and to talk all afternoon. And *then* we'll go get dinner and a show. Got it?"

I spluttered a little. "Umm, I'm going to get fat, Ms. Metabolism!" I put a mock-horrified hand over my mouth to cover my smile for dramatic effect.

"Honey, when I date a girl, I want to date a *girl*. Not a girl trapped in a little boy's body."

"Ohmigod. Did you just call me fat?" I exclaimed.

Clare rolled her eyes. "Get over yourself. You're gorgeous. See you tomorrow, Rain," she said flippantly. She stood, flipping her hair over her shoulder, and I watched her go in amazement.

Just as she got to the shop's front door, a huge deluge of sleet hit the ground, crackling hollowly in the night. I saw her shudder, that blank, lost stare seeping into her eyes again. But then she shook it off and blew me a kiss.

I sat, stunned, as the door closed behind her.

I overheard an old man behind me mutter gruffly, "Damn. All the hot ones bat for the other team."

I had just taken a sip of my coffee when he said that, and I was very glad Clare had already left as latte spewed from my mouth.

Yeah, *all* the hot ones bat for the other team. And then there was little derp me.

NINE

I SLEPT surprisingly well, despite my nerves jangling so forcefully that I literally thought I would shake out of bed. I didn't know if the jitters had come from the coffee or the promise of what Monday would bring.

At seven, my usual alarm went off. I blinked blearily for a moment, my nose chilled in the early morning air.

Just as I was stretching, my mom walked in with a huge robe pulled tightly around her. She smiled brightly at me and announced, "Go back to sleep. A huge ice storm hit last night. No school today because the power lines to the high school were knocked down. See you later, Raimi." She winked and left.

I got up and shuffled to my window. I pulled back the heavy velvet curtains and stared out the frosted panes. Everything was shiny like it was covered in a thin layer of glass. I smiled so big I thought my cheeks would burst. Clare was right. I took a flying leap back into bed and set my alarm for nine. Plenty of time to get ready for her.

I lay in bed, relishing that feeling of curling up under warm blankets when it's absolutely freezing outside. But what really delighted me, even more than no school, was the thought of getting Clare to myself all day long.

I BOUNDED down the stairs at exactly 9:59 a.m., right as our doorbell rang. Note to self: she was the punctual type. I threw the front door open, and Clare stood there shivering and grinning. Her white scarf tucked up around her chin made her flushed cheeks look even rosier. I smiled back.

She gave my bundled-up body a once over and laughed. "You do know how to dress for the cold, don't you?"

I had on my warmest jeans, tucked into sheepskin-lined boots. Under my fur-lined, black, button-up jacket was a black cashmere turtleneck, and to top it off I had wrapped a black knit scarf around my neck.

"What can I say? I'm from Texas! We don't do cold."

She danced casually down my sidewalk while I had to carefully hobble over the ice. Which in turn made her laugh freely. Clare was completely at ease, her white bubble jacket hiding yet somehow showcasing her slim, athletic figure. How she could walk in those stiletto boots of hers, I had no idea. She was like a Barbie angel, and I was just me. Me in black.

We got into her car, and for the second time, I sat in her passenger seat. Except this time, Clare wasn't crying and I wasn't trying to decide what to tell her and what was off the table.

I still didn't think I was ready to tell anyone about my gender transformation. Not even her. I comforted myself with the knowledge that she was holding things back from me, as well. Because that's healthy. Boundaries are good.

Clare distracted me from my heavy thoughts when she started fiddling with the radio just as we sped across an ice-encrusted bridge.

I couldn't help gasping. "Clare, if you could keep your eyes on the road when we go over icy bridges, that would be great for my blood pressure," I choked out, clutching my door handle tightly.

She laughed darkly. "Trust me. I'm not afraid of icy driving. If we're meant to die, it'll happen no matter how careful we are." And on that wonderful note, she turned the radio to an old jazz and swing station.

I raised an eyebrow. "Vintage?" I asked. "You?"

She nodded, her lips inexplicably tight.

"Hey, I didn't mean to offend you. I just didn't peg you for the type who liked jazz and swing music."

"There's a lot you don't know about me, Rain," she said huskily.

I laughed rather shakily and turned away so that she wouldn't see the monster blush that had crept across my face. This was going to be an interesting day. And I was going to love every minute of it.

When we got to the coffee house, she was out of the car and had my door open before I could protest. I scowled up at her. "I'm not helpless, you know. I could've gotten that."

She flashed a smile at me and caught my arm as I slipped on the icy concrete of the parking lot. Laughing, she replied, "Oh, I'm sure you were perfectly capable. But in the meantime, I still want you unbroken and intact. Well, for right now, at least." She winked, offering her arm.

I scowled even deeper and stopped in my tracks. "What gives?"

A delicate eyebrow arched reproachfully at my voice. "And by that you mean…." She trailed off, expecting me to fill in the blanks.

I fidgeted with my black gloves. "Why are you so ready to be out of the closet all of a sudden?" I breathed out in a rush.

She froze and dropped my arm. It took her a few seconds to recover from my question. Clare closed her eyes and took a deep gulp of the crisp air. "Because it's not like I can exactly go back in. And besides, once you find someone to come out for, it's not so hard."

I nodded slowly. That was a huge compliment she'd just given me, but…. "I… I'm not sure I'm ready to…. Well, at least not to the general public. I mean, you're awesome, but I don't think I can come out to everyone else. Not yet," I mumbled.

She nodded, her face filled with concern and empathy. "It's okay, Rain. I get it. I was exactly like that with my first girlfriend. I'm not going to push you to PDA with me. I'm a big girl. I'm ready to be out, but I get that you're not. I'll be here for you until you are," she said softly, a gust of wintry breeze blowing strands of golden hair across her face.

In that moment, we could have been the only two people on earth. I smiled, tears biting at the edge of my eyes. "Thank you. And of course, I'll be there for you at school. I think all of us have secrets we aren't ready to talk about. I guess you just have to choose your battles." I took a deep breath and added, "I'm not ashamed of being gay. I'm just scared of how people might react."

Her chilled, bare fingers brushed against my cheek, swiping away the tear that had made it halfway down my cheek. "No tears between us, okay? Of course, we all have secrets. And you shouldn't be ashamed of yours. You're perfect, Rain. Don't you forget that. You're perfect to me." And with that, she leaned forward and kissed me.

It wasn't this magical, fireworks-playing-in-the-background kind of kiss. It was just a simple brush of her chapped lips against mine. My eyes widened in surprise. Okay, make that shock.

It was just a goddamn kiss. And yet I knew that she meant it. I was happy. I was with her, and sparks were definitely flying between us. I smiled, and her turquoise eyes were alight as they looked into mine.

"You know, you have the prettiest brown eyes of maybe anyone I ever met."

She didn't say anything after that, just linked her arm in mine and helped me across the treacherous ice field that was the parking lot. There was a lot of giggling and teasing involved. Oh, and I made a complete dork of myself.

When we finally got inside, it was deserted. Thankfully. Clare marched up to the counter and ordered the same coffee for me that I'd drunk yesterday, slapping down money for us both before I could even get my wallet out.

I scowled again. "Would you stop it? I am a strong, independent woman who don't need no man."

She laughed so hard that she actually snorted, to her rather adorable embarrassment. I laughed even harder, loving the little quirks I kept discovering about her. Like how she twirled her hair when she was thinking and put it in her mouth without chewing on it. When she was trying not to laugh, she bit her lip. And my personal favorite was how she raised a hand to cover her mouth when she blushed. Which seemed to happen mainly when I complimented her.

We sat and talked for maybe an hour-and-a-half at the coffee shop. She talked all about her family. Her dad was a plastic surgeon and part-time pastor, and her mom was a valium-addicted, psychopathic housewife—her description, not mine. Apparently, having at least one screwed-up, dysfunctional parent was more common than I realized.

She was the only child. There'd been a brother who died before she was born, and she thought of herself as the replacement kid to keep mom from going totally off the deep end. Which sucked pretty hard. But it had the upside of daddy's disinterest, access to credit cards, and a complete lack of concern for her whereabouts.

Clare did talk a little bit about why she hadn't come out to her parents. Mainly the whole pastor thing, along with her aunt practically being disowned for being bi a number of years back….

All in all, Clare was almost as screwed up as I was. I even went so far as to say that to her.

"No way, hon. I got you topped," she snorted.

I raised an eyebrow, taking a careful sip of my coffee. "You underestimate me? Then you underestimate the twistedness of my upbringing," I said.

She put her elbows on the table, propping her head up, and studied me carefully. "Ever caught a parent on a substance-induced bender?" she quizzed.

"Yep."

She studied me for a moment. "Ever tried to kill yourself?"

Looks like she was going all-in on these questions. I squirmed a little in my chair.

"It's not something to be ashamed of. We all go through dark times, Rain. God knows I have," she sighed, blowing a piece of hair out of her face and sipping slowly at her coffee.

I shrugged. "I spent about six months in a seriously deep depression."

"Cut?" she asked quietly.

I met her eyes for a split second before looking away. "Yeah," I said, completely monotone.

"Same here, hon," she said casually, like we were talking about the odd weather phenomenon going on around us.

I really got the sense that she was seriously not going to judge me. And I prayed that she knew I wasn't going to judge her either.

She smiled slightly to herself, her lips barely tilting up. "Are you still a virgin?"

I coughed, spewing coffee everywhere.

Clare laughed musically and teased, "I'll take that as a yes."

"You would be right," I choked.

She leaned forward. "I'll tell you my first kiss if you'll tell me yours," she whispered secretively, even glancing around the room as if she was looking for anyone suspicious nearby who could hear.

I laughed nervously. "Okay, sure. You start."

She smiled, her face in deep thought. "Brad Heartman. Underneath a tree in broad daylight when I was twelve. I remember he had been teasing me about my new shorts. See, I was really dorky before I got so outrageously hot." She winked at me and continued, "But he was messing with me, saying my legs were so pale they were blinding him. I had gotten so upset with him that I ran away to hide under this tree and bawl my eyes out." Clare smiled, obviously deep in her memories.

"And when he got there and saw me crying, his face was absolutely priceless. He really had no idea how much he had hurt my little girl feelings. So he put his bike down and sat next to me, and before I could say anything, he leaned over and kissed me. It was really awkward, but it was really cute, too. I wonder if I should've known I was gay back then. I mean, I kinda did, but I wasn't sure what all my feelings meant, and I definitely wasn't going to say anything about my confusion to

71

him. Not then, anyway." Clare finished, her eyes zoning back in to present day.

I sat there, awed, for a minute. It was just a small slice of her life, but it was an intimate and personal one. And she'd shared it with *me*.

I smiled softly. "You know, you're really beautiful when you don't put up so many walls. I mean, you're still gorgeous when you have them up, but you just shine when you're vulnerable."

Clare covered her face again, a blush spreading across her cheeks. "Shh. Stop that. Stop being so sweet. Now your turn," she said, her cheeks flaming redder.

I laughed. "Just first kiss in general, right?" I clarified.

She nodded firmly, her eyes expectant.

I tried to remember back. And I was really glad that my first kiss's name could be taken as a boy's name. Things would've just gotten too complicated if that hadn't been the case. "Hmm. Okay, I remember. It was Reily Hann, sixth grade. At one of our school's cotillions, and we kissed at the end of the night. Outside the school on this little bench that everyone called the kissing bench because it was in the school's garden. It was also very cute," I finished smugly.

Clare nodded in approval. "Okay, first *lesbian* kiss." She said it like she was talking about the scandal of the century. I rolled my eyes, a blush flushing my cheeks hotly.

She squealed in delight at my reluctance and started her story. "Casey Adams. Three years ago. She was a senior, and I was a sophomore. But it's not that big a deal. I'm as old as a kid can be and still be in my grade. I was born like one day after the birthday cutoff. Anyways, it was in her room. It was maybe three o'clock in the morning, and we had both had a little to drink at this massive party at her house. She asked me up to her room because she had mentioned a *Star Wars* collection—

She broke off the tale to add as an aside, "And, if you haven't guessed it, I am the biggest *Star Wars* nerd on the face of the earth." She had to wait until my gales of laughter abated enough for me to hear her continue.

"Ha. Ha. You may laugh, but Casey didn't!" Clare stuck her tongue out at me as I struggled to contain my giggles.

"Back to Casey. This fancy *Star Wars* collection of hers consisted of a Luke Skywalker poster rolled up in her closet and a stuffed Yoda. Period. She said she'd just been looking for an excuse to "do this." And then she kissed me. At the time, I wished it had been more romantic. But, looking back, it was actually pretty perfect: just me, her, and the moonlight coming in through her window. As cheesy as that sounds," Clare finished, laughing.

But there was a real sadness brewing in her blue eyes that I didn't understand. I reached across the table and laced my fingers through hers. I started talking, trying to pull her from whatever it was she was reliving and *not* telling me about.

After a few seconds, she seemed to shrug off the melancholy and pinned me in my seat with a laser look. "Okay. Your turn."

"Mine was a little different. It was this girl I had only really just met. But damn, she was gorgeous. No offense, but honestly, the prettiest girl I had ever seen. And don't even get me started on her body. It's stupidly perfect. Anyway, we had only been talking for a little while. But I still felt as if I was getting to know her. I thought she was straight. I mean, she was with this asshole boyfriend that I had the urge to castrate on several occasions. She was off-limits, though. Until I sat in the car with her, watching it rain as she cried."

I took a deep breath and looked up at her just as she looked up at me. Two tears spilled over, one from each of her eyes, tracking down her face.

"Then this awful picture of her was all over the Internet, and it was all anyone could talk about. And I wasn't there for her like I should've been. I still feel pretty awful about that. But we all make mistakes. I honestly thought I had blown any chance with her when I met up with her by accident in a coffee shop. As for the kiss, though, well… it was perfect. Our lips were chapped, and it was freezing out. She kissed me, and it was the most innocent and sweet thing ever. And the rest is history."

I smiled a little, reaching out with my thumb to wipe a tear from her cheek.

"No tears, Clare. Because as long as you're with me, you should know just how perfect you are to me."

TEN

To GET into the pizza joint, we had to walk in through double glass doors and a tiny waiting area, then through a pair of hokey saloon doors on swinging hinges. The oak half doors opened with a chilly *swoosh* as Clare and I walked into the deserted restaurant.

I followed her, admiring how gracefully she walked. We slid into a booth tucked in the back. I settled onto the cracked vinyl seat, laughing as she bounced against the back of hers repeatedly.

Eventually, she sat still, but a modicum of nervousness remained in her eyes. It was like whenever she looked at me, she was completely intent on me but skittish at the same time. I could absolutely relate. I was still having trouble wrapping my brain around the idea of a girl like her being interested in a girl like me.

A cute waiter started toward us jauntily to take our orders. Clare's gaze narrowed dangerously as the waiter approached. But by the time he hovered over us, vulturelike, her expression had smoothed out. Had I imagined that flash of fury? Then Clare smiled up brightly at him, and I swear he nearly rocked back on his heels with the force of her beauty. She looked over the menu quickly, her gaze flicking from page to page. I grinned broadly as the waiter stared at her, his mouth agape. Poor guy was practically drooling.

"I'll have the triple threat pepperoni pizza with a side of breadsticks and cheese fries," she purred at him. I raised an eyebrow at her. I swear, she made ordering pizza sound like porn.

She shrugged and replied a little defensively, "Brad hated it when I weighed more than he wanted me to. He really got on my case about how I looked the past few months." She added a little wistfully, "I've missed carbs."

I recoiled mentally in horror. Brad thought Clare was fat? Shut the front door! What an idiot. I looked over the menu as the waiter cleared his throat and interjected a little awkwardly, "I don't see how any guy could complain about you."

Clare threw back her head and laughed in what sounded like genuine amusement.

The waiter smiled triumphantly and started scribbling something on his little notepad. I craned my head to see what he was doing and caught the beginnings of a phone number. I felt bad for him. Clare was jacking him around, but I didn't understand why. I mean, I could understand her being in a pretty severe man-hating phase right about then, but the Clare I knew wasn't intentionally hurtful to other people.

"Boys are crazy," she declared. But then she looked up at him sidelong, smiling a little. "No offense," she drawled.

I literally thought the waiter was going to melt into a puddle at her feet. I tried to catch her eye, to silently ask what the hell she was doing, but she assiduously avoided looking over at me. Confused as hell, I kept looking through the menu, glad for having an excuse to look anywhere else but at the two of them flirting aggressively with each other.

"I dunno. I think girls are crazier. No offense." The waiter retorted with a grin, ripping the sheet of paper from his pad.

He had the unfortunate timing to set it down exactly when Clare reached out to trail her fingers softly, suggestively, over mine. I giggled a little—I have to admit it was as much in embarrassment as anything else. What the hell game was she playing at? She'd promised me no public displays of affection that would start any rumors.

The waiter snatched up the paper and crumpled it in a tight little ball that he jammed into his back pocket.

Clare turned to the waiter. "Yeah, but girls are a good crazy. Well, in my world at least," she murmured.

The waiter scowled, his lips pressed into an angry white line. It was evident that she had just dealt a major blow to his ego. The poor guy just got cockblocked by a chick who didn't actually like cock.

I tried to look sympathetically at the waiter, but he wouldn't meet my gaze at all. I finally mumbled, "I'll have the garden salad with a side of fruit."

He nodded wordlessly and wrote down my order.

Clare smacked my arm hard enough to make me drop the menu. "Hey!" I protested.

She laughed and tugged on the waiter's sleeve. He looked equal parts freaked and reluctant. She pulled down on his sleeve until she could grab his shirt collar and force him close enough for her to put her mouth practically on his ear. She whispered something, and his eyes went wide in some combination of surprise, fear, and nervousness.

He jerked upright as she turned his shirt loose and took a quick step back from her. He turned and all but ran for the kitchen.

I waited until he was out of earshot to demand, "What the hell was that?"

She answered breezily, a little *too* breezily, "Oh, please. It's just what you get for trying to be healthy. I ordered you some actual food."

I threw her one of my mother's don't-bullshit-me stares.

She exhaled hard. "Fine. I admit it. I was screwing with that guy's head."

My mouth opened in disbelief. "But why?"

Instead of the lighthearted response I expected, she murmured rather darkly, "That's Chase Housen. Have you met him yet? Do you know what he did to my friend, Mira, last year?"

I shook my head no in response to both questions. I never had been the world's best at staying on top of the latest teen gossip.

Clare played with the straw in her glass of ice water. "He roofied her. Where do you think Brad got them to drug me? That's his supplier," she said quietly.

Holy crap. In retrospect, I had to say Clare had actually taken it pretty easy on him just now. I'd have kicked the guy in the junk if I'd known.

Clare turned her head to look out the window. Everything was icy, and without the comforting blanket of white that snow brings, it all looked cold and dead, oddly preserved like a sick museum. As we both stared out the window in silence, it started to sleet a little, a winter shower of frozen pellets beating down. I was starting to half believe her claim that she controlled the weather.

She finally broke the silence, her breath puffing against the glass. "I know not all guys are creepy, psycho, sex-driven rapists. But I certainly have a knack for collecting the ones who are around me." Her sardonic smile froze on her lips, her eyes reflecting intense pain that didn't match the smile. She whispered so low I barely heard her, "Maybe that's part of why I like girls."

My eyes softened as I gazed on her. She looked so small and vulnerable and hurt in that moment of raw honesty. Her slender shoulders hunched under the bulky bubble jacket. I slid slowly out of my seat, moving like she was a wild creature I was trying hard not to frighten into bolting. I took off my jacket, unwrapped my scarf, and tugged my hands free of my gloves. Still moving with extreme caution, I slid into the booth next to her. My reflection joined hers in the big pane of glass.

I rested my hand very lightly on her shoulder and spoke carefully. "Sometimes, it's not about the cards we're dealt. Sometimes, it's about how well we bluff. It sucks that you had to be with Brad for so long. But that's over and done with. Not all guys are bad, I swear. People are people. It doesn't matter what gender they are. There are just as many creepy, psycho, sex-driven rapist girls as there are guys. It all depends on the individual person."

Someone must have turned on cheesy Italian music in a back room, because without warning, it started crooning through a hidden speaker system. So we sat there, me with my hand on her shoulder, her staring out the window, just letting her work stuff out in her head, while a dopey song about "*amore*" echoed around us.

Eventually, she reached up and pulled her scarf off, followed by her jacket. Underneath, she had on a simple, long-sleeved white camisole. It was slightly see-through, and I caught a glance of something on her left hipbone. I poked it playfully.

"You didn't tell me you had a tattoo," I teased.

Clare shrugged, her eyes clouding over. She replied vacantly, "You never asked."

I wrapped an arm around her shoulder and squeezed. "Hey. Look at me. Whatever it is, let it go. It's done, and you seriously can't change a thing that's happened in the past. So be here with me, instead. I'll bet you a million dollars it's a lot more pleasant than what's rattling around in your head, right now. Okay?"

She nodded, slowly retreating from her daze. Luckily, the waiter came just then with two heaping, steaming, huge plates of greasy goodness. He plopped the plates in front of us and fled without saying a word to us. Smart boy.

I covered my mouth in horror as I stared down at the giant mound of pasta before me. "Oh my God, Clare. I cannot eat a whole damn plate of whatever it is you ordered me. I'm getting sick to my stomach just looking at all of that."

She laughed wickedly. "Don't worry, I'll help you."

The waiter came back to the table with my salad and her pizza. "Anything else I can get you?" he asked reluctantly.

Clare shrugged and replied, "You never know when I might need to get something from you."

Was she hinting that she might want to buy drugs from him sometime? Who in the hell was she planning to roofie? Alarmed, I watched as the jerk actually grinned at Clare and tossed the balled-up paper with his number onto our table.

She smiled brightly at him until he turned around. And then she neatly placed the paper onto the lit candle in front of us. Clare shivered almost perceptibly as the ashes quietly sifted and settled to the bottom of the tiny pool of wax. I didn't look up to see if Chase had spotted her burning his number. I was more interested in watching Clare and the way pain morphed into satisfaction in her eyes as she watched that fire burn.

There was more to Clare than I knew. I was sure of that. But there was also more to me than she knew. So I couldn't say anything except hope that someday we would be ready to share all with each other. We ate in the comfortable drone of Italian music, downing enough food to keep us bloated for the next three days, and basked in each other's comforting company.

All in all, it was pretty nice.

Eventually, we grabbed our coats and scarves and headed out in a postpizza coma. Chase tried to flirt with Clare again as we were leaving the restaurant, and I barely managed to drag her out before she kicked his shin or assaulted him outright. How could one guy's ego be so huge that he didn't realize the mortal danger he was in by attempting to get into Clare's pants after what he'd had a part in doing to her?

Honestly, I wouldn't have minded her tearing off some important body part or two of his. I understood where she was coming from. But I was selfish enough not to want to see her end up in jail for the rest of my time in high school.

How she could be even halfway civil to Brad's buddies, or to any of the dozens or hundreds of kids who'd known Brad was blackmailing her and not done anything to help her, I had no idea. She was one strong human being, that was for sure. The more I saw of the shell she put up around herself and the barriers she positioned between herself and others, the more honored and special I felt that she had let me in.

As we strolled past the restaurant's front windows, she swung her arm over my shoulders and whispered in my ear, "Chase is watching this, and knowing him, he's having some pretty nasty fantasies."

Blushing furiously, I snorted and whispered back, "Or maybe he's just constipated."

She laughed, looking back at his nearly cross-eyed lust as he watched us saunter past. She tossed her head once, in contempt. We didn't bother giving him a second glance after that.

We reached her car and got in. We had to sit a couple of minutes for it to heat up enough to defog the windows, and then she eased out into the street. I was glad to see Clare taking the road with more caution as we wound our way back toward home. The clock on her dash read 5:25 p.m.

I whistled softly. "We've killed seven-and-a-half hours together."

Her lips turned up slightly. "Time flies when you're having fun." Her voice was quiet in the crisp air of her car.

We drove for nearly a half hour to get to the other side of town. It would normally only take ten minutes or so, but the ice had slowed everything down. I loved it. It made life a lot calmer, like it was all moving by at half speed. And I got to live it with her.

She parked her car in the early twilight, overlooking a semifrozen creek behind the second restaurant she was taking me to. I took everything in.

The clouds had broken enough for the sun to peek out at us from behind the western hills past town. What must be a lush forest in the summer was now a tangle of bare black trunks covered in a layer of crystal before us, seemingly dripping with golden water, although it was only ice being lit by the fading sun. The one thing missing was a fluffy layer of snow on the ground, but, otherwise, this was the dream of winter I never saw in Texas. I wanted to frame this moment with Clare, capture it in one perfect memory, and keep this picture in my mind and heart forever.

Clare turned off her car, and we sat together as cold whispered into the car. She let out a soft puff of air that hung white in front of us. I smiled and tried to catch it playfully in my hand. She beamed lazily over at me. I caught her gaze in the dying sunlight. Her eyes looked silver, devoid of color, despite their vivid hue in daylight. I swear, she looked like an angel. I made another memory to add to the first one.

She spoke slowly, reflectively. "You know, every Christmas my mom would sober up enough to make cookies with my dad and me. One year, we burned a batch and I cried. It must have been ten at night, quite the late hour for ten-year-old me. But my mom just smiled and told me to make another batch, all by myself. She said that I was ready to do it, and I didn't believe her."

I held my breath, not understanding yet why this story was important to her, but I could feel its significance.

She continued, "I remember that she knelt down in front of me and took my shoulders in her hands. She looked me straight in the eye and told me that, eventually, all of us grow up. And when we do grow up, we have to do things and make decisions on our own. The trick is to have enough experience, to have made the same batch of cookies enough before, to get it right. I remember she whispered in my ear that I would do the cookies absolutely perfectly because she knew I had made enough batches of cookies in my life to get it right this time."

"And did you?" I asked in a hush.

"She and dad went to bed, and I made the best damn cookies I have ever eaten. Of course, I ate them all. I was too old for Santa to still be real." Clare took a big breath. "I guess what I'm trying to say is that I think I finally found the right recipe. I know how many times I had to burn the cookies, how many times I thought I'd found the wrong Rain. I really do," she finished in a rush, peeking up nervously at me through her long lashes.

I smiled and leaned forward to murmur nervously myself, "Clare. I've never made cookies before."

The breath caught in her throat before she replied so low I barely heard her, "Then let me teach you."

We strode proudly into the tiny diner. It was completely fifties-themed with everything from a checkered floor to waitresses in poodle skirts. I glanced reluctantly at Clare from across our little chrome table.

"I don't think I can eat another bite. I'm in a total salt and grease overload."

She didn't say anything, just waved the nearest rollerblade-adorned waitress over.

"If you could bring us the kitchen sink for two, that would be awesome."

The waitress nodded, her curls bouncing. She smiled over at me. "Anything else I can get you young ladies?" Her voice was weathered with age.

I started to shake my head when an idea popped into my mind. "Oh, my gosh. Do you serve hot chocolate?"

"Only the best stuff in town. Two mugs coming up."

I beamed at her. "Thanks!"

And with that, she skated back over to the counter where the waitresses were placing their orders. The diner was surprisingly packed with couples or a group of friends at nearly every table and booth. Clare had snagged us the last table, so all that was left in the entire place was a booth near the door.

Of course, it was just our luck that Brad walked in at that moment with a girl on his arm. Not just any girl, either. He was with Cam.

I nearly peed myself.

ELEVEN

CAM'S JAW hit the floor the minute she saw Clare and me together. It didn't help that in the waitress' absence, Clare had been playing with my hand. I'm pretty sure I was whiter than a sheet of scared paper at that point.

Brad just smiled, though. I didn't get it until I saw what he was smirking at. Clare was as white as I was, and they were having an obvious staring contest. Except this one wasn't friendly in any shape, form, or fashion. I had to make a decision then and there. Because that closet door was getting pretty damn flimsy.

I unglued my gaze from a shocked Cam and squeezed Clare's fingers, keeping her from sliding them away. Clare broke eye contact with Brad, her eyes locking on mine.

She only mouthed three words. "Are you sure?"

I nodded, taking Clare's hand with both of mine. I kept her eyes hostage so she wouldn't look past me. I even resisted looking at Brad and Cam in the reflection of the windows opposite them.

"So how did you find this place?" I murmured, more urgently than the subject would've usually warranted.

"Brad brought me here," she answered in an equally intense tone.

"And now he's bringing his latest girl here, too?" I gave one short bark of laughter and asked toxically, "Doesn't he know a guy has to change his MO between victims? Does he even have two brain cells to rub together?"

Clare threw me a grim look. "He's smart. And if you don't think he is, then he hasn't turned his full attention on you yet. Because when he does, there basically isn't anything he doesn't think through and plan for. Trust me," she said flatly.

"I do," I said quietly.

Clare smiled slightly, and the waitress saved us by bringing over arguably the biggest mugs I had ever seen in my life. They looked like buckets with handles. I broke into a totally goofy grin as she set down the drink and its monstrous mound of whipped cream and chocolate drizzle in front of me.

Clare gaped openmouthed at hers. "Everyone said the hot chocolate here was big but… I never thought it was *this* big."

The waitress chuckled, skating casually away. I took a small sip from a chocolate straw and was rewarded with a shot of pure whipped cream. I groaned orgasmically.

Clare nearly choked on her hot chocolate "Oh my God, Rain, you did not just go there."

"And yet it would seem I did," I deadpanned.

She laughed, attracting the attention of a few nearby tables. But we didn't care at that point and were trying hard to forget about everyone else around us.

We tried, that is, until Brad strode boldly over to our table. "S'up, dykes?" he said bluntly, loudly, and without shame.

I wanted so bad to just punch him in the balls. I really didn't think anyone would be offended, I mean, c'mon. It was *Brad*.

Instead, I just smiled up at him syrup-sweetly. "Hey, Brad. Great to see you, honeybunches," I drawled in my best Texas twang. I even batted my eyelashes for effect. I took a long, deliberate suck on my chocolate straw while Clare visibly collected herself. I hoped she was taking courage from my open contempt for her ex.

Brad inhaled sharply, enough air to effectively puff his chest up about like a rooster.

Clare murmured sweetly, "Careful, babe, you might hurt yourself if you try to be any more manly. I mean really, I'm just quaking in my boots."

I didn't bother to keep my voice down. "So. This is the guy who was so bad in bed he turned you gay, huh, Clare?"

"You have no idea. Atrocious. Thirty-second wonder on a good day," she replied equally volubly.

Brad blustered for a minute, seemingly at a complete loss for words at our boldness.

I smacked my lips and smiled over at Clare. "Tell me, Clare. Are you offended by his little greeting? Personally, I'm not. I mean, hey, girls are great! What's not to love about 'em?" I gently disengaged my hands from hers so I could lean back to stare up at Brad coldly.

He ground out from behind clenched teeth, "I swear to God, Clare, leaving me was the worst decision you ever made. I'll do whatever it takes to make your life a living hell. I'll even tell your parents."

Her eyes flickered with worry for just a second before she laughed without humor. "Go right ahead. It would save me a lot of trouble. Why don't you go back to your date? I'm already sympathetic for your next victim."

Brad slammed his hands down so hard on the table that both of our hot chocolates spilled. We danced out of the way of the steaming liquid as the waitress whizzed over to us, towel in hand. She shot Brad an irritated look and started mopping up our table.

We did our best to help her as the waitress addressed Brad sternly. "I'm sure your parents would be disappointed to know about all the girls you've brought in here, and all those little pills you slip into their drinks." She finished cleaning up the worst of our table and pulled out another towel to continue mopping.

"I never did any such thing," Brad protested angrily.

I smiled up at him knowingly, sipping at my remaining hot chocolate. He glared at me like he was seriously contemplating killing me right then and there. I would've liked to see him try.

The waitress shook a finger under his nose. "Don't lie to me, young man. I've known your parents for nigh on forty years. Two things are going to happen in the next two minutes, or your parents are going to get a phone call from me. First, you're going to go up to the register and pay for these girls' drinks that you spilled. Second, you're going to take whoever that poor girl over there is home. And you're not welcome to come back in here again." The waitress said it all matter-of-factly, like she was informing him that the sky was blue.

I struggled desperately not to laugh, but Clare made no such effort. Brad spluttered a few seconds before storming over to the counter and yanking out his wallet angrily. Silently, I thanked fate or whatever had put that waitress here in this diner today. Who knows how violent Brad would've been willing to get with us. Let's just say I wasn't eager to find out.

I looked over at Clare as she intently watched Brad and Cam leave. Cam glanced over her shoulder poisonously at me. I shrugged. Too bad I didn't care. But Clare was definitely rattled. I was glad when our waitress/angel skated back over to us with two new hot chocolates.

She smiled down at us and squeezed Clare's shoulder supportively. "You two listen to me. Never pay any attention to that boy or anyone like him. They're all just bitter and scared because they don't understand. And people have a way of being mad when they don't understand something."

Clare blinked rapidly a few times before looking up at her. "Thank you," she said quietly. "For everything."

The waitress nodded curtly. "I'm just doing what's right. Now enjoy your night and enjoy the weather for goodness sakes."

I smiled and reached out for Clare's hand. She flashed me a huge smile. The waitress skated away. I looked out the window and gasped. Big, fat, white flurries of snow floated down. It was absolutely gorgeous.

"I hope you like ice cream," Clare sang.

A smile broke across my face. "Almost as much as I love snow."

TWELVE

I HONESTLY thought I was going to explode with the amount of ice cream Clare and I consumed. She rubbed her stomach shamelessly, leaning back in her chair and letting out a big sigh.

"Class in a glass, Clare, class in a glass," I mused.

She grinned. "What can I say? I'm an upscale lady."

I toyed with my spoon, dragging it through the remaining mishmash of ice cream flavors.

Clare joined me, her spoon clattering noisily against mine. "Hey! I thought we agreed that I would get all the vanilla variants."

I laughed and scooped up a big spoonful just to annoy her.

"I like a girl with some sass," she murmured.

I nodded a little sleepily, entering the first stages of sugar crashing, and it looked as if Clare wasn't very far behind me. Our energy was definitely starting to abate, and anyway, our movie started in twenty minutes.

We tried to pay for our ice cream and drinks, but the waitress very casually explained to us that Brad had already paid for us both. In full. I started to giggle and was laughing nearly hysterically by the time we got to Clare's car. I sagged in the passenger's seat. I was exhausted physically, emotionally, and mentally. Brad's little visit had made more of an impression than I had realized. Or than I wanted to admit. Clare seemed to be right there with me.

The drive to the theater was silent but not in an awkward "I really don't know what to say now" way. It was actually really comfortable. I just watched it snow, honestly. I didn't know what it was about snow, but it just felt like I was supposed to be quiet as it fell.

We trudged through the white wet slush into the theater, bought tickets, flopped into seats, and promptly fell asleep.

I WOKE up, my ear resting on top of Clare's head. She had her head tucked into my shoulder and was still asleep. The end credits were rolling as I blinked groggily at the screen. I breathed a small laugh. Her hair fanned out over me. I blew a strand of it from my face, and her eyes fluttered open.

The annoying part was that her makeup was still perfect. I mean, c'mon for goodness sakes! She slowly rolled off of me, rubbing her eyes *and still not freaking smearing her makeup.* We looked at each other and smiled sleepily. Clumsily, our feet found their way down the stairs and out of the theater. So much for the big finale of the evening.

Her car crunched along the icy streets, snow smacking into her windshield outside. Swing music filled the interior. It was truly surreal. When we got to my house, we just sat for a little bit, watching it snow. By then, it had snowed at least four inches.

"You know, in all the years I've lived here, it's never been so eerily perfect," she said reverently. I swung my head around to look at her. Clare shrugged. "I always felt like something was missing. And then Casey... well, Casey happened, and I knew what had been missing. But I always felt out of place before that, you know? Like I was living in the wrong skin."

"I know exactly how you feel," I replied fervently.

She nodded. "In a lot of ways, Brad's like all this snow. He was always covering me, stifling me, burying the real me. But, I guess I let him smother me. And that's my fault," Clare confessed.

I reached over and took her cold hand in mine. "No. Brad is not your fault. And feeling like you're in the wrong skin isn't bad. It's normal. Part of growing up. It's burning the cookies a million damn times until you get it right. And then we spend the rest of our lives trying to figure out what made that one batch work so well."

Her lips tilted up in a half smile. "What if instead of questioning it, we all just took the recipe for what it was and left it alone to do what it did?"

I snickered. "Well, that's not going to happen because people are nosy by nature."

Clare chuckled slightly. "As my daddy would say, 'amen.'" Her voice was clear through the night's quiet.

She was right. Being here with her was eerie. But it was also pretty perfect. After a few more minutes of idle chitchat, I opened the car door reluctantly. My parents would start asking questions before too much longer, so I decided to save ourselves the trouble and call it a night. She walked me to the door silently. It continued to snow steadily, nestling into both my and Clare's hair.

We stood in front of my door for a few seconds before she leaned in silently. Brushing a strand of hair out of my face, she kissed me. Not an innocent peck but an actual kiss. I think I melted a little bit. I closed my eyes, enjoying it.

She pulled back, her lips turning up. "That's how I should have kissed you the first time," Clare whispered, and my breath caught.

"Look at you, son!" my dad bellowed. I whipped around, breaking the spell that had fallen over us. He was grinning down at me drunkenly. One eye wasn't focusing properly as he stood hulking in the doorway. There was a bottle of whiskey in one hand, the door in the other.

Clare laughed musically from behind me. "Jesus. And I thought my mom's benders were bad. Anyway, I had a great time with you, Rain. See you tomorrow!" Clare called, walking down my steps.

I'm pretty sure I choked a good-bye out, but I was too terrified to remember much after that point.

When my dad closed the front door behind me, I followed him into his office where he collapsed onto the leather sofa with his damned bottle. I must have yelled at him for a good five minutes. It's not worth going into the details, but I let out a lot of resentment that had been building for a while.

He just blinked up at me, took the last swig of whiskey in the bottle, and started bawling. I stared down at him. And then I went upstairs and started crying. Maybe it was just an emotional release of my own, or maybe it was a reaction to seeing my dad in such a god-awful state. Or maybe it was because of the single text message waiting for me on my cell phone.

You're going to pay for that stunt at the diner. You and her both.

I hated that my dad was a drunk.

I hated that he had called me son in front of Clare.

I hated that Clare didn't know the truth.

I hated being afraid that Brad would find out I was trans.

I hated that I was more afraid of Clare finding out from him.

I hated that I couldn't have just been born into the right body.

But hate doesn't get you anything except a night that started out lovely only being remembered bitterly.

THIRTEEN

TUESDAY MORNING dawned bright and early, a normal start to a normal day. Seven inches of snow had fallen over the course of last night, blanketing everything in a comfortable white fluff.

My mom came upstairs around seven thirty to make sure I was awake, and inform me that work crews had miraculously corrected the electricity problem at the high school despite the crappy weather. I assured her that I was not only awake but plenty capable of driving myself to school. Her concern was touching, nonetheless, and I was glad to see that she and Zach had made it home safely from wherever it was they had gone for the weekend.

It might seem odd to you that I wouldn't know where my only sibling and virtually my only parent had gone for an entire twenty-four hours, but it honestly didn't bother me. My mom would occasionally just take Zach out on a mother-son day trip, stay somewhere, and then fly right home. I didn't question it because she had done exactly the same thing with me when I had been little. I guess we all needed a break from Dad, sometimes. Not that I don't love him... most of the time.

I shrugged on my jacket, readjusting my book bag over it. I tugged at my shirt, staring at the mirror. When I looked out my frosty window, my eyes reflected coldly. Every now and again, I would look into a mirror and jump back a little bit in shock at who was staring back. And I mean shock in the best way possible.

My lips turned up in a smile as the thought of seeing Clare crossed my mind. But along with that came the reality that I would also have to see Cam and Brad—possibly together—today. A flood of unknowns inundated me, from Freddie's reaction to the two of them, to possible rumors the two of them would have already spread about me and Clare.

The drive from my house to the high school had never seemed longer. Neither had it ever felt so short.

I SLID into my first period seat relatively unnoticed, considering Brad and his friends hadn't gotten to class yet. I shuffled my notes around nervously, doing some last minute cramming for a Spanish test we were taking today. There were only three other people in the class with me at that point, and I was grateful for the quiet. Everyone was silent as we all studied. Students trickled in over the next few minutes in various layers of clothing. I was starting to worry Clare would be late or worse, not show, as the clock kept ticking. But she didn't disappoint me.

Looking like her normal, perfect self once again, she strode into the class with the same confident air she always had. People did a double take as she walked straight up to me and took the seat beside mine.

She smiled at me coyly, and I returned the favor. Yep, if I'd had any hope of staying in the closet, it was shattered right then and there as whispers filled the room. And it only got worse when Brad strolled in surrounded by his normal group of brutes. Clare and I quizzed each other in preparation for the test, trying to ignore Brad. He was calling our names, along with a lot of the other students.

I gritted my teeth and turned over the next flashcard. Thankfully, the teacher walked in. She whirled around like a crazy bird all over the classroom, reminding us of all the material that was going to be covered on our test.

I can honestly say that taking that test was a total and complete relief. I shot out of the Spanish classroom the minute the bell rang,

Clare and I went to our respective second period classes alone. I avoided Brad and Cam for the rest of the morning, dodging them whenever possible in the halls. It wasn't easy, and it was clear that the word about Clare and me was very much common knowledge by fourth period.

By the time lunch came, I was ready to collapse in relief next to Freddie. He held out a chair for me and then stood up and pulled one out for Clare. I seriously wanted to cry. He smiled reassuringly at both of us, and I saw the sadness in his deep brown eyes. I put my hand on his shoulder. "I'm sorry about Cam. I saw her with Brad last night. It's stupid of her to pick him over you. Really stupid," I murmured.

He shook his head. "No, I mean it makes perfect sense. He's Brad Heartman, and I'm just me. I'm not an athlete or popular. But she's happy, so that's all that matters."

Clare cleared her throat from behind me, and I turned, surprised, in my seat to face her. She was smiling a bit awkwardly. It was the most out of place I had ever seen her look.

"Erm, I don't mean to intrude, but you're wrong, Freddie. She'll think she's happy with him for a little bit, but then she'll realize what she's gotten herself into. And it's hard to get away from him if he really wants to keep you. Believe me," she said solemnly.

Freddie just looked at her for a minute before nodding slowly in understanding.

And at that exact moment, the two of them walked in. Cam was draped over Brad like a toga on a frat boy. He had an arm around her waist possessively.

Freddie recoiled as if he had been hit. I felt bad for the poor guy.

Cam sneered at us from across the room as Brad whispered something in her ear. She smiled and tilted her head ever so slightly in response, never once breaking eye contact with Clare and me. They started strolling across the cafeteria like a royal couple on processional. They were perfectly in sync as they took each step. As they drew even with our table, the two of them paused like a well-practiced routine.

Time slowed to a standstill as Cam reached into her back pocket and drew out a can of something. Clare and I didn't even have time to react as she pointed at us and let loose, spraying us with silly string. It was sticky, clinging to my hair and clothes. Cam was pretty good at evenly distributing the goo between Clare and me.

I screamed like a total girl and was completely caught off guard.

Freddie rushed to get napkins as Clare and I shook off all that we could. I let it fall to the floor, each florescent string trailing like the accusations they were. Without speaking, I reached over to get a long string off of Clare's head.

I was still carefully picking it out of her hair as Brad snarled, "This is what happens when you're a useless fag."

Without looking away from Clare's hair, I knew Brad had walked away because I could hear the click of Cam's boots against the cold tile. Freddie hurried back with more napkins. It was mostly futile at this point. If it was going to come off, it already had. And if it hadn't... well, I hear silly string is the new black.

No one in the cafeteria said a word. They all just went back to eating their meals in silence. I didn't have it in me to be offended. I was too busy, and I was too tired. Anger is a useless emotion, anyway. Although right then, it would have felt pretty damn good.

CLARE AND I went home without talking to each other. After school, I didn't look back as my car rolled out of the student parking lot. She was at cheer practice, and there was no one worth looking back at.

The night was a blur of homework after the teachers suddenly decided it was a good time to start assigning mountains of work. It was a good distraction, though. Especially when a series of six messages came through on my phone from a blocked number. I deleted them without looking.

FOURTEEN

IT WAS a late night of homework. So much so that when I finally lifted my head from my math, the first rays of sunlight were beginning to brave the frigid landscape. I sighed as my hands flew to my face. I was to that point of sleep deprivation that it was hard to believe my face was still attached. Fascinating face. Just fascinating.

I staggered into my shower, the warm water flowing easily down my body. I felt my muscles begin to relax, tension knots from bending over countless textbooks starting to loosen. I washed my hair slowly, savoring every moment of escape I had in this little oasis. I sagged against the tiled wall when I turned the water stream off and shook my hair out softly.

The hum of a heater somewhere in the distance echoed against my foggy shower door. I stepped out one foot at a time. No need to rush it. I was exhausted, anyway.

But when I looked in the mirror, my tired mind began to sharpen in the haze of humidity. I find that unpleasant memories have a way of coming back to me, no matter how I try to avoid them. No matter how I felt or what had happened lately. The memories found a way into my head regardless of whether or not I wanted them to.

I sighed, my thoughts drifting back to before my transformation. It had been absolutely awful. I shivered, thinking about the first time I had looked in the mirror and realized that it shouldn't have been a boy staring back at me. I had just stood there and cried until I accepted it. And it had been hard.

For the longest time, I was angry. I would date girls just to prove to myself that I was a guy. I'd make out with them to show myself how manly I was. It made sense at the time, I swear.

When that didn't work, I turned to a razor and to pain to show myself that I had control. But the only control I had then was the control to stop, and I didn't. Not until my mom walked in on me, passed out from pain pills. She took me to the hospital, since my dad had been overseas on business. My little brother had been there when I woke up, and he asked me why I was so sad and why Mommy had been crying. I'd shrugged.

It had all been in the suicide note I left on my chest for my parents to find. Little did I know that my mom had been up all night researching gender reassignment and therapy to help me get into the body I belonged in.

I stared into the mirror now, putting a hand to my face to feel that it was all still real. The memory of that morning after was too vivid for me to ever forget. And I never wanted to.

My mom had strode in, coffee in both hands. She told my little brother to sit outside until we were done talking. She had smiled at me, given me my drink, and stroked my hair. Her fingers had been gentle but no gentler than before. And she had matter-of-factly explained how my father had set aside a $100,000 trust fund for me last night, even though he was still in Germany. She told me that I was going to see the best doctors in the country, and that we were going to get through this together.

She had looked me in the eyes and said, "I'm so sorry I couldn't give birth to you in the right body. But we're going to take care of it, and don't you ever dare think this is something bad or to be ashamed of. We are who we are, and it doesn't matter what anyone else says. Always be you, and your father and I will be here for you."

I swear she must have rehearsed that with a psychologist because it completely calmed me down, and I never worried about being afraid of myself again. I didn't really think it was rehearsed—I honestly just think my mom is that great. My dad had always been a little wary of how to treat me once I started hormone therapy and surgery, but I knew he loved me. And that was enough.

Here's the thing about gender that most people don't seem to understand. It's not about what body you're in or what body you're attracted to. It's about what's in your head. So, your genetics could say one thing, but how you act, how you think, how you were *supposed* to be, might say something very different.

I was lucky to be born into such an accepting family, but I didn't dare question it. Everyone has a different journey to take, but in the end, it doesn't matter how you get to where you're going. That's what I said at support groups, anyway.

I finished getting ready for school that morning in thoughtful silence. Because as much as I was beginning to love this new town and starting to fall for someone, it still nagged at me. Clare didn't know about the whole being born a boy thing. I wanted to tell her. Except something magical happened. It was like someone had sewed my lips together. And I wasn't in a hurry to break free either.

I guess there's more than one way to be trapped.

FIFTEEN

SLEEP DEPRIVED and with a very large cup of coffee in my hand, I walked into Spanish. I couldn't help but laugh. There was a message in sharpie hastily scrawled on my desk.

Dyke sits here.

Original. I rolled my eyes as Brad snickered. I took the seat without trying to clean it up. Instead, I took out my classwork, shrugged, and said, "Hey, Brad. So tell me more about how it feels to be so sexually frustrated. I mean, that must suck. Seriously, man, I feel bad for you." I nodded sympathetically at him.

The class stared at me. And then they stared at Brad. Obviously looking for his next clever comeback or lack thereof.

Brad nodded, a slow and very ugly smile sliding over his lips. "You know. It's a good thing you aren't a guy; otherwise, you would be laid out on the floor right now," he growled.

I barked out a short peal of laughter. I was just opening my mouth to snap at him when Clare breezed in, coffee in hand. It was clear the homework monster hadn't been limited to the juniors last night.

She sighed heavily at Brad. "Don't worry, everybody. He's just trying to make up for his exceptionally small dick. Really, all his posturing and bravado is just overcompensation. I wouldn't take it too seriously."

Clare never broke pitch. It was as if she had just told us what the weather was like outside and all of that was perfectly normal to say. I

99

thought Brad was going to explode. So, in other words, I was really amused.

"Yeah, you would know!" Brad shouted at her before thinking. Immediately, a dark blush started to seep into his cheeks. The class snickered despite his nearly Cro-Magnon growl.

Clare took her seat next to me and winked. We hadn't gotten even with him, but that had felt good. I know, I know. Higher road, blah blah. Be the bigger person, blah blah. The bottom line is that karma can be quite entertaining if you aren't on the receiving end of it.

The day flew by, a mishmash of tests and laughter barely concealed about Clare and me. I ignored it as best I could, and I have to say, Freddie helped. He walked us to our respective classes without complaint or wavering. It was a small blessing, but a blessing, nonetheless. I slogged through my homework that night and Thursday, a constant grind of more and more projects.

I think what surprised me the most was how quiet the situation with Brad stayed. There were no more big showdowns, no more big displays of an assertion of power or disapproval. It was quiet. Spooky, almost.

I made it all of the way through Friday, thinking things had finally taken a turn for the better. The students had seemed to have started their process of coming to terms with us, letting go, and eventually a state of normalcy. And by normalcy, I mean not giving a shit about anyone else's problems. Normal is good. So I had deluded myself pretty effectively when I was leaving late again after helping out in art. Then I heard it.

Like some sort of twist on the past, I heard her crying. Her breaths were short and labored, covered by stifled sobs. I would have recognized her voice anywhere.

I broke into a sprint down the hall, bursting through the only, ironically, possible place the sounds could be coming from. She was in the book room, wedged in a corner between two very empty and very dusty bookshelves. Her face was hidden behind her hair, successfully concealed from anyone walking by. Her long limbs were folded in around her brokenly.

I dropped my bag carelessly on the floor, my thoughts focused solely on Clare. She was sobbing so hard she didn't even know I was there until I put a hand on her knee.

Her face turned up to meet my gaze. Puffy eyes, chapped lips, and a runny nose met me. Her mascara was only barely smudged, but it seemed that she had scrubbed off all of her eyeliner in the process of losing it. She was a total train wreck, and it still took me a minute to shake off the shock of how pretty she was. Her eyes were even bluer when she cried. It just wasn't fair.

I squeezed her knee. "Hey. What's wrong?" I murmured, tucking a piece of hair behind her ear.

She made a distraught sound at me but didn't utter a word.

I took her chin in my hand and made her meet my eyes. "I'm right here. Talk to me."

I nearly lost my balance when she threw herself on me. Wrapping her arms around my neck, she let loose with a semihysterical scream. I hugged her tightly, not letting go as I maneuvered her to rest more comfortably against the cold, cinder block wall. She cried for a while, maybe five more minutes of heart-wrenching sobs that eventually abated to only an occasional hiccup.

When she was finally composed enough, I tried again. "What's wrong, Clare?" I didn't have even the slightest idea what was up. If Brad had laid a single finger on her, I swear to God—

"Bigot parents have bigot children," she mumbled shakily. Her voice was froggy and cracked. But it was hers. There was at least ice to break now. I nodded, putting another piece of hair behind her ear as she pulled back from me and leaned heavily against the wall.

"Well… yeah," I mused.

A half smile crawled over her face. "Guess who finally got involved? The loving parents of Little. There's a joke in there somewhere."

Aww, jeez. I let my fingers lace familiarly through hers. She squeezed them briefly before letting go. I heard the clock ticking loudly in the background as I waited for her tell me the rest in the empty room.

"Some of the parents of the other girls on the cheerleading squad have requested that I be kicked off. Put on probation. Boiled in holy water. Whatever it is, it doesn't matter. The message is that they don't want devil's spawn around their perfect, angelic little darlings. I guess they're afraid the gay will rub off on them."

Her words were so angry, so poisonous I actually had to lean back a little to absorb them.

She smiled cynically at me. "Isn't this town just great? My mom is probably so bent right now she wouldn't remember my name. No, she might know my name. Maybe not who I am, though," Clare spit out, letting it all sink in around me.

I shook my head, a fire starting to burn in my stomach. "They can't do this! The school board would get sued into the next century, and we would all be on the six o'clock news. They won't go through with it."

Clare just nodded, completely passive. I almost didn't recognize this Clare, so drained of her fight. I put my arm around her, not allowing her to wiggle away this time. I kissed her on the cheek. She tasted like salt. I laid my head in between her neck and head.

"Coach told me that my parents might have to get involved. She's trying to keep that from happening. I think she's on my side. I hope she is. She told me that I'm her head girl, and that I'm not going anywhere. I even believed her," Clare murmured.

I could feel the vibration of every word through her throat. "So why don't you believe her?" I echoed hollowly.

"Because I heard some of what the parents are saying. They're talking about going to my father, the pastor, and suggesting that I be sent to a special facility. I think it's supposed to pray the gay away."

Giggles erupted from deep down in my belly. I couldn't help them. This stupidity reminded me so much of my own upbringing that I found it genuinely *funny*.

"And while you're there, make sure you find a good Christian boy to marry so you can get started on your family. Gotta get cracking.

You might have to get cured again if the gay is really strong in you. Kinda like a possession," I said in my best southern drawl.

Clare hiccupped a few choked gurgles of a laugh out. Another big sigh from her raised my head up momentarily, but then I settled back onto her neck. I wasn't going anywhere.

"Rain, do you know what would happen if my dad found out? I can't even begin to fathom…. If he couldn't pray the gay away, then I would be a liability. And he would take care of it. Send me to a mental institution, get me medication, disown me, for God's sake. And, even if my mom could find a way to cope with it, that would require being sober. Not her forte."

The air grew warmer around us as she spoke, but cold sleet started pinging down against the roof. Sounds and senses filled my mind. The room smelled like oak and cedar. Clare smelled like sweat, tears, and something sweet like vanilla. Sleet and her breathing are what filled my ears along with the rush of my frantic heartbeat pounding against my eardrums. I wanted to curl up in a ball and take Clare with me to protect her from everything. But the only thing I could give her were words and promises I might not be able to keep. And secrets. I could give Clare a lot of secrets.

"Well, you could always come live with us. My mom would flip for a little bit about staying in separate rooms, and then she'd be cool. She's out of town on business now, but she'll be back Monday. I'm sure we could—"

Clare's phone rang. Hastily, she fished it from the bottom of her giant purse. Her eyes widened ever so slightly when she read the caller ID. I peeked over her shoulder and saw what was awaiting her on the other end of the line.

Dad.

I heard yelling through the phone and a lot more profanity than you would think a pastor would ever dream of using.

Clare winced, tears claiming her eyes once again. "I'm sorry, Daddy—" She broke off.

He had cut her words in half. I held her tighter to me as words like hell, faith, disappointment, useless, worthless, and evil hung in the air between us like little individual nooses. I was gaining a new respect for my family's exceedingly quick acceptance. When the phone call finished, Clare blinked back tears and just stared at her screen for a minute.

I wrapped my free hand around her. "My parents are out of town. If you want to crash at my house, just let me know," I murmured.

Her lips slid into the barest half smile I had seen in my life. "That depends. Do you have booze?"

I snorted, kissing her lightly on the cheek. "Are you kidding me? My dad has an entire man cave devoted to just that. And a flat screen TV that will blow your mind."

I GLANCED into my rearview mirror to see Clare's car following me faithfully up my driveway. I tapped my fingers impatiently on the steering wheel as the garage door opened as slowly as mechanically possible. Finally, I pulled into the far left, Clare taking the far right spot. That left a space between us. And I wasn't sure it was just distance anymore. We walked into my house quietly, my sneakers the only occasional squeak of sound around us. I turned on the lights in the kitchen and started looking through the fridge.

"Do you want anything to eat?" I asked as Clare took a seat on our counter.

"Ice cream?" she mumbled.

I laughed. "Sorry, don't have any."

"Pizza?"

"Don't have that, either."

"Candy?"

"Sorry."

"Chocolate?"

"I'm starting to see a trend here."

She laughed then, the tiniest hint of a giggle. "I think we need a shopping trip."

I watched as her eyes lit up and then dimmed sharply, filling with tears. My eyebrows shot up. "Let me get my coat."

Clare blinked a few times. "I wasn't serious. I'm fine," she said wryly.

I rolled my eyes, sighing heavily. "In the women's dictionary, 'fine' does not exist. Now get your coat or freeze, but either way you're coming with me, and we're going to buy all the junk food we want.

"And we aren't going to care one single little bit about anything else," I said with finality.

SIXTEEN

WHEN WE got back to my house, I could actually feel the fat starting to settle onto my thighs, and we hadn't even started eating yet. Basically, if you could name a junk food available in our local store, we now owned it. I took a long slurp from an energy drink, discarding all thoughts of caloric intake and possible morbid obesity. Oh, well, calories don't count when you're with someone else.

Clare popped the top off of her raspberry ice cream and immediately went to my mom's blender. She spooned in half of the carton, then turned to ask me, "Where's the booze, honey bunches?"

I stood there, letting the decision set in. "Are you sure you want to do this, Clare? You know alcohol is a depressant, and it's really not a good idea to layer a depressant on top of being sad," I said logically.

She started laughing, not with humor but bitterly, her laughter sour with anger. "I'm positive. Get me drunk, Rain. Get me really, damningly, drunk."

She followed my heavy footsteps into my dad's man cave. It really was an impressive set up. The room was easily as big as our family room. When you entered, the plush carpet led down three stairs into an almost basement-like setup. I padded down those stairs and switched on the florescent lighting.

Clare giggled from behind me. "What, no disco lights?" she teased.

I sighed and flipped another switch. The florescent lights lowered to a deep purple before changing color. The lights kept changing, going through the rainbow in a surreal '80s way. I continued down the stairs, my feet sinking into the deep shag carpeting. In the middle of the room was an iridescent chandelier that threw colored shards of light over the huge pool table. The wall facing us was completely covered in mirrors, and the two sidewalls were covered in every sort of fermented liquid you could imagine. Jack Daniels, assorted schnapps, every type of vodka ever made, malts from around the world, and any age scotch you could dream of. It was drunk-heaven down here.

Clare was loving it. She stood in the middle of the room and turned in a slow, delighted pirouette. "Oh my God. Your dad is a pimp, and you never told me?"

I choked on my laughter. "No, no, Clare. He is not a pimp. I swear."

She snorted as she turned a small dial on the wall. Soft music began to pump in around us. "You've got to be shitting me," she breathed.

I sighed. Dubstep. My dad's latest obsession was Dubstep. I figured it was his manopause kicking in, but Clare obviously had other ideas.

"Not only is your dad a pimp, he has legitimate bitches. I want to meet them," she demanded.

I rolled my eyes, but I could see why anyone looking at this room would think that. I perched myself on the pool table and opened my arms. "Mis bebidas alcohólicas es el alcohol," I said, not sure if I said it right.

Clare seemed unconcerned with anything but the very long row of liqueur bottles in front of her. My dad must have had forty different flavors of liqueurs, varying from orange to licorice, to cookie dough flavored.

She exclaimed, "Oh, damn. You have coffee liqueur? I love that stuff!" She took the bottle down off the shelf. Her slender fingers snaked around bottle neck after bottle neck until her arms were full of goodies. She glanced up at me. "Aren't you going to get anything?"

I shook my head. Permanent designated driver's status is a hard thing to leave behind. Not to mention that I worried a little about what would happen if one of us didn't stay reasonably sober and self-controlled.

Clare threw her hair back with gales of laughter. "Oh, Rain, Rain, Rain. That's it! Grab yourself some vodka, honey, we're making Jell-O shots."

I shrugged and hopped to my feet to leave.

"Nope. No leaving until we have some vodka to play with. My arms are full. You have to grab it for me. Go on, now. I'm not going to talk to you until you fetch the happy juice." And with that, she pressed her lips tightly together and looked expectantly at me.

I felt myself flush as I made my way over to the vodka. I picked one at random. Vanilla vodka? With Jell-O? I thought not. I put it back and searched a little before settling on plain old Russian vodka, trying to keep it as classy as possible. I trudged out of my dad's room, turning off the lights and music as we left.

"You know, Clare, I'm starting to think you're a bad influence."

Her peals of her laugher bounced back in on me from the walls. "That's what they all tell me. But then they get drunk and love me, anyway. So it's kind of a karmic wash."

It turned out that Clare wasn't as much of a lightweight at drinking as she painted herself to be. She explained to me about her heavy Russian and German roots as she poured the coffee liqueur over her ice cream in the blender. Clare added ice to the blender, then picked up the bottle again, studying it carefully. After a moment's contemplation, she took a deep swig from the bottle. A grimace passed over her features, no doubt from the sharp burn of alcohol down her throat.

I did the responsible thing and took the bottle away.

She scowled at me and switched on the blender. As it whirred in the background, she declared, "We need music."

I pointed her to my parents' massive stereo. Clare plugged her iPod in and, surprisingly, cued up an indie playlist. I raised an eyebrow at her. *What happened to the jazz and swing?*

She answered my unspoken question. "I save the oldies for when I want to remember." Her voice was melancholy, serious, almost lost in the down-tempo harmony.

Remember what? I watched her stride over to the blender and stick a straw straight into the oddly colored brew. She sucked down a considerable amount at a fairly alarming rate.

"Slow down, there, kiddo," I said disapprovingly, trying to coax the blender from her hands.

She shook a reproving finger at me. "Didn't your mama ever teach you manners?"

I shook my head and gave up on separating her from her high-octane milkshake. I opened the freezer and grabbed my own carton of chocolate ice cream. I hopped onto one of the barstools, pulled my knees up to my chest, and started picking at my ice cream. We stayed there in silence for a few moments, Clare not speaking until she'd downed the rest of her concoction and broken into an Irish malt whiskey and tossed back a couple of shots.

"Better?" I murmured.

She nodded, her cheeks starting to flush with the beginnings of a buzz. "Yep. Definitely."

It wasn't pleasant just sitting there, watching her mix drink after drink. What was interesting was that between drinks, I spied the beginning of tears forming at the edges of her eyes. But then, as the acrid burn of alcohol hit the back of her throat, the tears would clear away.

I couldn't bear to see her drink herself into oblivion like my dad did every night. I eventually had to separate myself from my own semipanicked feelings and observe her in a clinical, objective way. As she finished a glass of orange juice and vodka, I finally spoke up.

"You done yet?" I asked grudgingly.

She nodded, as she swallowed the last bit of poison that so dominated my dad's life. "Yep. A lot better now."

I had to give her credit for holding her booze well. Her enunciation and pronunciation were absolutely perfect. Her hand snaked out and popped open a bag of Doritos. She ate a good chunk of the bag before starting in on a bag of Cheetos.

"Want to talk about it?" I asked, scraping the last bit of ice cream from my pint carton.

"No."

I nodded, picking up the discarded Doritos. I crunched through a few, not tasting anything. "But you need to. Talk about it, that is. Like it or not. So spill," I ordered.

Clare shook her head. But at least this time when the tears pricked her eyes, she didn't reach for booze to stop them.

"I can't, Raimi. I just can't."

I snorted. "Yes, you can. Don't lie to me or to yourself. It's a waste of our time."

Her eyes swam behind a sheen of tears like melting turquoise. Her shoulders shook with unshed sobs, held back by her tightly pressed-together lips. Watching her cry in complete silence like this was like watching humanity without a human. It was awful. It was empty.

I moved over to her, taking her hand in mine and hugging her. She was cold to the touch. Lifeless. All I could think was, this was how a corpse must feel.

"My dad is planning on sending me to rehab in Mississippi. To pray the gay away is exactly how he described it. Actually, he said a lot of things."

Her voice ripped through the silence she'd cloaked herself in, breaking my train of thought. How in the hell could any parent intentionally cause their only child this kind of pain?

110

She continued, her words more gasps of pain than sound. "He told me I was going to hell. That I was broken and a disgrace and wrong and a Satanist."

I wrapped my arms around her. My fingers dug so deeply into her shoulders that I could feel her frantic pulse. No, she didn't feel like a corpse. She felt like someone who wished she were a corpse.

"He said that whatever demon had taken his baby from him would be exorcised, and that he promised he would get his little girl back, no matter what the cost," she whispered. Her tears spilled down my arms, tracking down us both.

I held her tighter.

She clutched her fists at my back, clinging to me as desperately as I was hanging on to her. "My mom lives on painkillers, day and night. She pops them around the clock like some sort of zombie. Literally. The only time I see her is every four hours when she comes into the kitchen and takes her pills. Then she just goes back into her bedroom. My parents haven't slept in the same bed for years." Clare continued on, her voice gradually losing emotion. I got scared when her pulse started to slow.

"I told my mom I was gay the night the picture was posted. She would see it anyway. I told her I was gay, and she just looked at me like I didn't really exist. She didn't even say a word. She just looked at me as if she could see right through me and took her damned pills. Then she left me standing there alone in the kitchen. She just left, like she was too tired to care."

I buried my face in her collarbone. My tears slid down her skin. I was crying for her. Because I knew I had to tell her tonight. There could be no more hiding between us. No more secrets. I guess once you cry on someone, there isn't really an option to go back.

"Oh, Clare," I whispered.

Her chest heaved against me, and she shoved me off. "No, I don't want your sympathy." She wiped angrily at her face. Even after all the drinking she had done, her words were perfect, without any hint of a slur. "I don't want it, Rain. You and your perfect family. You with your perfect mom, your perfect brother, even your perfect alcoholic dad. You don't even know what you have," she shouted, her voice striking me like a slap.

I stood there and took it, not letting her words sink in. She was drunk. She didn't mean it. Her eyes boiled, the melted turquoise heating and hardening like lava. The stereo stuttered in the background. Clare took a step toward me. She raised her hand as if she were going to hit me.

I clenched my face, my body, my entire being in preparation.

And instead of hitting me, she knotted her hand in my hair and kissed me as frantically as she could. Her mouth found mine, begging for me.

I returned her urgency as best I could. It was hard to keep up with her passion, her hand holding my back strongly. I wrapped my arms around her, settling against her. It wasn't like anything I had ever experienced. Our first kiss had been innocent. Our second kiss had been romantic. We had kissed since then, but nothing like this. This was raw. It was something… more. The salt of her tears and the taste of vodka on her lips mingled in a way that was distinctly *Clare.* I don't think I'll ever forget how she tasted that night.

Eventually we parted for air, our lungs heaving against each other. Once the fog of heat subsided, only one thought made its way across my mind. I squinched my eyes closed, trying to shove it away. I could still feel her lips on mine as warm tracks slid down my cheeks.

Clare settled her head into my neck and sighed. "Tell me, Rain. Whatever your big secret is, you can tell me," she whispered, her lips tickling against my skin.

Goose bumps shivered down my arms. I didn't say anything.

"Please," Clare breathed.

I swallowed hard. She kissed my neck.

I couldn't think then. The only thing I could feel was her and me and the secrets and her taste and the music and everything. I felt everything. I felt her. And it all poured out. Everything. From Texas up until this very moment, I told her everything.

She kept her arms around my neck the entire time.

When I finished I let out a huge, shuddering breath. "I'm sorry I didn't tell you," I murmured.

Her breath washed over my skin. Clare's laughter brought a deep numbness into my throat. After everything, she was going to leave me. I braced myself for the blow. I wished she had hit me. It would have made things easier. Safer.

But falling in love isn't something you can do safely. It's something you don't even realize you're doing until you're already too far gone to turn back.

Clare sighed and kissed my neck again. "Never stop surprising me, Raimi. It's the best part of being with you."

I don't know how long we kissed or when we curled up on the couch and fell asleep together. We didn't have sex. We just fell asleep in a pile like a couple of puppies. I drifted into sleep from the safety of her arms, her head resting on a pillow and my leg thrown across one of hers. She toyed with my hair as dreams claimed us both. I don't think I had ever slept so soundly.

WHEN I woke up the next morning, Clare was absent. The smell of eggs wafted in from the other room. Saturday morning cartoons were playing on the TV. I sat up and ran my hands through my hair.

"Morning, sleepy head." Clare's voice drifted in to me from the kitchen.

I smiled over at her and stood. I lazily made my way toward her, taking some orange juice from the fridge. I let my mind sift through the events of last night. I took a swig of juice from the carton, Clare's voice droning in my head, casually.

"You're going to have to fill me in on the details of last night. It's a little hazy."

I put the carton down, confused. "What do you mean?" I asked wryly. I took note of the empty coffee packets poking out of the trash and went to the cupboard to pull out an actual glass. I carefully poured myself a serving of orange juice. For lack of anything else to do with my restless hands, I took a sip of it.

"I mean that I don't remember anything from last night," she elaborated.

The glass nearly slipped from my fingers. I didn't say anything. Numbness seeped into every inch of my body.

"It's weird," she commented, blithely unaware of my horror. "I haven't blacked out like that in months. Well, more like years. Oh, well. It's not like we would've talked about anything important last night while I was drunk off my ass," she said flippantly.

I thought I was going to faint. But instead, I took another drink from my glass, wishing fervently that the juice was spiked with vodka.

"No. You didn't miss anything," I whispered.

SEVENTEEN

I DON'T remember the rest of that weekend. Whenever I try to pull up the memories, there's nothing there. Just empty, numb space. Monday morning, I woke up with another note taped to my pillow. It was just like her first note, her swirling handwriting scrawled messily across the page.

> *Rain,*
>
> *Thanks so much for letting me stay this weekend. Didn't know you could drink that much! Anyways, I went home early this morning to get clothes. I'm going to have to face the music sooner than later. See you in Spanish!*
>
> *Hugs and kisses, Clare*

I rubbed my eyes, puffy from crying. I didn't remember crying. But then again, I didn't remember drinking. And it was clear I had done plenty of that. I made myself coffee before stepping into a scalding shower. The hot water flowed over my limbs. It was then that I started shaking.

A few brief snippets of memory flashed through my mind at a time. A glimpse of Clare's hair. The taste of shots sliding down my throat. Kissing Clare good night. They all mashed together into a Technicolor collage of a weekend I would probably always wish I could remember. Only one thing definitely stuck out about it—an Eiffel Tower shooting up off a two-dimensional plane.

I had told Clare I was trans. *And she hadn't remembered it the next morning.* I would put money on that being the reason why I had been drinking. I slid to the floor of my shower, hugged my knees to my chest, and cried. I cried because she didn't remember. I cried because my parents still weren't home to care. I cried because I had been in a stressful situation and done the one thing I promised myself I would never do. I cried because I had acted just like my dad. And I cried because there were seven new messages from Brad. I didn't know what they were about. But I was terrified I might have drunk texted him back.

God only knew what I could've told him. When I got out of the shower, I turned my phone off. I didn't want to see what Brad had to say. At this point, I didn't even know if it mattered anymore. I hoped it didn't.

SCHOOL WAS a zoo. Apparently, a big party got busted, and ten seniors had been arrested over the weekend for various charges, including DUI, underage drinking, and a few counts of date rape. I hung close to Clare when we entered the cafeteria, scared of what we would find. Cam had her arms around Brad, comforting him, I assumed. Her eyes bored into mine like fire, shooting daggers in my general direction. It wasn't until I sat down that I realized it wasn't me who she had been glaring at. It was Freddie who had walked in behind us.

Shauna was only too eager to spill all the good gossip to Clare and me as we sat down at our usual table.

"Brad's friend Mark had the party of a century this weekend. It makes the biggest party we've had this year look like a kid's birthday. There were at least six dealers at the party. Nothing heavy like meth, but they had ecstasy, roofies, pot, acid, painkillers, and I heard a few rumors about coke."

Clare's lips pursed as someone handed her a scribbled list of the kids who had been arrested. She showed the list to me, making a point of jabbing a finger at one name in particular on the list.

The waiter from the pizza joint. The guy who provided roofies to most of the high school boys in town. Clare smiled grimly and mouthed *karma* to me. I nodded.

Freddie looked like he hadn't slept in days, his cheeks hollow and bruised with sleep deprivation.

Shauna leaned in closer to us to whisper, "Freddie is the one who called the cops. A girl overdosed, so he called 911. When the police got there, they found like three other kids overdosed. He saved their lives. But in the meantime, he's going to be known as the kid who narked."

Freddie glanced over at us from the lunch line, and I sent him an encouraging smile. But he didn't meet my eyes.

Brad got up to meet him in the middle of the cafeteria, and I flinched for Freddie.

"You actually thought you had a right to show up to school today?" Brad screamed, the veins in his neck standing out starkly. Cam put a hand on Brad's bicep to steady him. He shook her off.

Shauna leaned over to me one last time. "Brad's little brother, Cory, was one of the kids who overdosed. And his older brother was the one dealing ecstasy. It's a miracle Brad didn't get charged with anything. God knows how hard it must have been for him to find someone sober enough to drive him home."

Clare inhaled sharply and turned her eyes on Shauna. "But Cory is only fifteen. How in the hell did Brad manage to get him into a senior party? I mean I know Brad's his brother and all, but still. There's a reason freshmen aren't allowed to come to the big parties!" she declared fiercely.

Shauna nodded. "Exactly. Brad is the one who got him in. Jesus, that's got to be one helluva family dynamic. Oldest child supplies middle child's habit. Middle child gets youngest child into a party where oldest child then gives him access to what youngest child uses to

117

overdose. This is why America is failing as a country." She shook her head in disgust.

I turned my gaze back to Freddie.

"You are one low son of a bitch to think you can walk back into *my* school like this," Brad yelled.

I scanned the crowd. No teachers in sight. And it wasn't like Freddie could respond or try to get help. Then he would really be forever labeled a narc. Instead, he just stood there, clenching and unclenching his fists. Even though Freddie was taller than Brad, Brad had a definite weight and strength advantage over him.

Everyone, including me, waited anxiously on the edge of their seats. We were all anticipating something. But none of us knew what.

And then it happened. Brad punched Freddie hard in the gut, and as Freddie doubled over, Brad slammed his fist into his face. Freddie obviously was having problems breathing. Brad obviously didn't care, and obviously wasn't done. Brad kneed Freddie mercilessly in the groin.

I wanted to do something, anything, but I swear my body was stuck in place. So in other words, as I watched my friend get pummeled, I didn't do anything. I really was on a roll with this whole inaction thing. No one moved to stop Brad.

And then it got weird.

Clare sprang from her seat at the same time Cam did. You would expect Clare to go to Freddie, and Cam to Brad. Except the exact opposite happened. Clare threw herself at Brad, giving him a huge restraining bear hug. Cam grabbed Freddie by his shirt and pulled him away from Brad, her hands pulling desperately at him to make him stand upright.

Clare eventually had to literally jump onto Brad piggyback style to get him to stop thrashing. I watched her lips brush against his fiercely, talking him down desperately.

I clenched my fists to keep my own anger from running away with me. I never knew I was the jealous type until then. But the longer I saw Clare draped all over Brad, the deeper the pit in my stomach sank.

I couldn't take it. I tore my gaze away from them and focused my stare on Cam and Freddie.

Freddie looked utterly in shock. Cam was pounding her fists against his chest. I couldn't hear what she was saying, but she was crying like he had died. He eventually grabbed her wrists and held her there. She looked up at him, her hair falling carelessly around her face. Freddie's thumb ran over the back of her palms. I saw his lips move before he pressed them to her forehead. Cam closed her eyes, tracks of tears silently streaming down her cheeks. She folded in against him, and he hugged her. His nose was bleeding and his eye was already starting to puff up.

Even though his entire body must have been in terrible pain, he still held her. I watched them carefully. It was an interesting show in the social dynamics of human beings. The entire cafeteria was taking it all in avidly right along with me.

Freddie and Cam had known each other since they could walk. I thought back to all of the idle touches they shared at lunch, from Freddie brushing her hair back to Cam stealing food off of his plate. Everyone else had known that they had a thing, but they had apparently never admitted it to themselves or to one another.

I wanted to say that as I saw them, Freddie softly stroking her hair and back to calm her down, that I felt happiness for them. But I didn't. All I felt and all I saw was the pain Cam had put him through.

She had left him the minute the opportunity presented itself. She hadn't thought about him or how it might affect him. She just left without a second glance back, not even a good-bye.

And yet, Freddie had still waited for her. He knew that Brad was higher on the social ladder and that Cam had left him behind to try to climb that social ladder. But he didn't care. He'd waited for her all the same. So when she finally came back to him, *he* comforted *her*.

And there he was. Right out in front of God and everyone in the whole school, holding her. Consoling her. Probably whispering to her that it would all be okay.

That's all love is, though, isn't it? Someone always gives more in a relationship, and someone is always taking all they can get. It really does beg the question of which one was which in my own relationship with Clare. What were we each looking for in a relationship? More important, however, was the question of what were we taking from each other.

I turned my gaze back to Clare and Brad. She was off of him now, standing in front of him, staring him down.

All I could decipher from their body language was that Clare was really upset with him and that Brad was just as upset with her. Clare tossed her hands up in frustration and exasperation. Brad ran his hands through his hair and eventually held his hands behind his neck in that jock-y way guys do. Clare pinched the bridge of her nose and sighed heavily, her shoulders bobbing up and down. They kept talking, and I continued to observe and make assumptions that I shouldn't have made.

But that didn't stop me from doing it.

Because when I looked at them together, I saw the history. They were each other's first kisses under a tree in a park after he made fun of her. They had watched each other literally grow up. Brad presumably had no idea Clare was a lesbian. But then, Clare probably didn't know she was a lesbian, either.

No matter what crappy blackmail he'd pulled on her, and no matter what twisted crap he'd forced her to do with him, the fact remained that their history together was important.

History always means something to people and to everyone around them. Even though Clare and I were in a newer relationship, she still had no idea the depth of my secrets or how much of my past I was keeping from her. Not that I'd tried to keep it from her. Or at least, she didn't remember that I had tried to tell her any of it.

Guilt overwhelmed me, taking over all of my senses and drowning me in a twisted agony of lying to someone I was falling in love with. I was going to throw up if I stayed here any longer, watching the rawness of everything around me.

When I realized that I truly couldn't handle it, I stood up. I imagine a few people turned to watch me leave. A lot of people didn't, though. I walked out of the cafeteria without looking back. I brushed past a teacher who was sprinting toward the cafeteria. And I didn't look back.

Just like Cam, I didn't look back.

EIGHTEEN

BRAD GOT suspended for three weeks. He was due back Friday. As in tomorrow, Friday. I hadn't talked to Clare since the fight in the cafeteria.

She left me three voice mails the first week, sent me fourteen texts, and six e-mails. The second week, she left one voice mail, five texts, and two e-mails. She didn't leave me anything on the third week.

It was probably for the best, anyway. Clare deserved to be with someone who could be honest with her. Someone she could trust completely without the worry of hidden secrets. She was the kind of person who needed someone to steady her, to be a rock for her.

And I was the kind of person who needed someone to be steady for me. Being with her was like tying two sailboats together in the middle of the ocean during a hurricane. When neither of us had anything to hang on to, we sank. If one of us went under, so would the other.

In those nearly three weeks of separation, Cam and Freddie had finally gotten together. Good for them. Freddie would balance Cam out nicely. He was good at being her rock. I was starting to suspect he had been there for her a lot longer than any of us knew.

In my absence, Clare had thrown herself back into cheerleading. The other cheer parents hadn't taken action to actually kick her off the team, and I doubted anyone would be able to beat her out for the job of head cheerleader fairly. She had been captain three years straight for a reason.

Everyone was whispering around the school about her now notorious drinking binges. Clare was developing a reputation for getting absolutely wasted at every party she went to. Not like that overtook her main reputation, of course. She was pretty well known as the class gay.

But, to her credit, she was owning it and not taking crap from anyone. If we were still dating, I would've been 100 percent proud of showing her off to the rest of the school. Then again, I also wouldn't have let her drink as much as she apparently was.

And as for me, I hadn't really done anything revolutionary or life changing in the past three weeks. Other than throwing myself into my art, I hadn't spectacularly remodeled my identity. No, all of my thoughts were going into brush strokes, lighting, and saturation values and all of that stuff that nonartists don't really give a crap about.

My grades surprisingly weren't suffering. In fact, they had gone up, if only very slightly. I can't say it enough. Art was where I channeled all of the emotions and numbness of the recent drama.

I didn't even know what to call what had happened between me and Clare. There was no formal breakup. I just stopped talking to her. So I guess it would be accurate to say it was me who bitch-froze her out. It was for the best, though.

I wasn't what she needed. And I was afraid of what would happen if I told her the truth. I had no idea how she would take it. The one time I told her, she was probably too drunk to decipher left from right. Honestly, that night still remained mostly lost in the fog of all the drinking I had apparently done that weekend.

There were a lot of reasons I had stopped talking to Clare. All of them seemed perfectly justifiable in my head at the time. And they were still valid in my mind going on three weeks later.

I was convinced I was doing the right thing for both of us. I refused to admit that it was because I was afraid. Afraid of myself and afraid of the truth. Once again, I had backed myself into the closet. Except now, I had no intention of ever coming out of it.

So it was that, Thursday afternoon, I was once again holed up in the art room after school.

I didn't hear her footsteps. She had a way of being light on her feet at all times, like she was ready to run from us all at any second. I was too intent on my canvas to see her. I had my ear buds in, blasting music into my skull, almost making my jaw rattle along with the beat.

I was almost done with the painting. It really was beautiful, and it was very clearly the best painting I had ever done. It was my favorite memory of all time, committed to canvas. Of course, it had to do with Clare. When an artist takes inspiration from something that means a lot to them personally, it usually turns out pretty well. And if the artist adds emotions on top of that personal significance, the end product is pretty much guaranteed to be fantastic.

She tapped me on my shoulder. I jumped about an inch off of my stool in surprise. I looked up into turquoise eyes, and a chill washed over me.

Very deliberately, I set my palette and brushes down on a nearby counter. I padded over to the sink and washed my hands—which was a bit of a project since I was painting in oils. I had to pull out the paint remover to get it out from under my fingernails. The whole time, she just stood there, still. Waiting.

When my hands were finally clean, I took my ear buds out carefully and paused my music. I was out of delaying tactics.

Reluctantly, I looked up at Clare. Her hair was straightened, hanging down her back in a smooth veil of blonde. It looked as soft as it always did. Since the cafeteria, though, her face had gotten harder and colder with every passing day.

How was I still managing to convince myself that our being apart was for the best?

My canvas was turned away from her and I was glad she couldn't see it. It would've hurt too much if she had. I breathed deeply and leaned against the paint-smattered counter.

"What?" I said icily.

Clare just looked at me. Then, "Wow. You really are a bitch, aren't you?"

Her tone of voice was poisonous. But her words hurt like a punch in the gut. I forced myself not to wince outwardly. This was better for her. She was leaving for college in a few months, anyways. It wasn't like we would last that long. I was protecting her from being further hurt.

Still, I didn't want her to think that the person who helped her get through finally coming out had been lying to her all along.

"Yep. I am," I said.

I really was a bitch for doing this. I gritted my teeth. *For the best, for the best, for the best.* The words chanted through my head over and over again.

She turned toward the door, and I started to exhale in relief. But then she stopped, whipped around, and glared at me venomously. "You know, I really thought you cared about me. But I guess you lied about that the entire time."

I blanched at that. Darn it, I was trying to prove to her that I hadn't lied to her the entire time. That was the whole point of not talking to her.

As the ramifications of what I had done started to sink in, Clare resumed walking to the door. I panicked. I didn't want to lose her. I *couldn't* lose her. I couldn't.

"Wait!" I called out.

She kept walking.

I snatched my painting from the easel and took off after her. I stepped directly in her path in the hallway. She sidestepped me, but I grabbed her wrist. She twisted away from me defensively, her mouth opening to no doubt tell me off. And then her angry glare found the painting.

Her breath caught, and she just stared at it. Her hand went limp in my grasp as she stopped struggling. I saw the tears well up in her eyes.

"I cared about you, Clare. I still do. But I just couldn't keep hurting you. I'm not the kind of person you need. You need someone strong, someone who can be steady for you. Someone like—"

She cut me off midword and kissed me. I was starting to see a pattern to her preferred method of shutting me up. Not that I was complaining. She pulled back, and my hand dropped from her wrist.

Clare ran a finger over the edge of the canvas. She lifted her gaze to me slowly, maybe even hesitantly. "You weren't hurting me, Rain. I don't know where you got that idea from."

I took a deep breath to explain to her that I had been doing just that, but she put a finger to my lips. "No. Listen. I don't know where you got this idea that I need someone stable. Maybe I do. But needing something and loving something are two different things. And I was starting to love you. The only thing you did to hurt me was leave me."

I identified a bunch of different emotions all tangled up in her voice. I heard anger, sadness, and something else. Something heavier and deeper than the rest of it that I couldn't put a name to.

She let out a faintly exasperated laugh, a sound I hadn't heard in a while. I hadn't realized I had missed it so much until I heard it again.

Clare took the painting gingerly from my hand, murmuring. "This really is beautiful, you know."

I nodded, looking at it once again. Clare was right. It was beautiful.

It was a familiar scene to us both. It was a painting of a parking lot, cars smudged and distorted in the background because of the snow. Everything was coated in a thin layer of white, dusting down. And in the middle of the canvas were two girls kissing. A tall blonde and a small brunette. I had painted our first kiss.

If I wasn't mistaken, tension was starting to build back up in Clare's shoulders. "What I don't understand is how you can paint something like this, but you can't bring yourself to even acknowledge my existence for three weeks. Do you even know how much that sucked for me?" Steel edged her words. She turned her gaze on me, her eyes burning with anger.

I pursed my lips and didn't say anything for a long time. A string of swearing erupted inside my head. Finally, I drew in a big breath. "I was protecting you from the truth. From the truth about me," I finished in a rush.

She laughed again. But this time it was a bitter sound devoid of humor.

"Oh really, Rain? So the world revolves around you? Well guess what, you weren't the only one keeping secrets. But I didn't end the damn relationship because I was afraid of something you didn't even know about." Her voice rose until she was practically shouting. Her face was flushed, not only from the anger but from the tears forming in her eyes again.

"You don't understand." I whispered. I bit my lip and looked away from her. I didn't want her to see me this way, and I didn't want to see her like that, either. There was a storm brewing behind her eyes, and I didn't want to see it when it broke.

"Of course, I don't understand! Of course, I don't understand, because you won't tell me anything. You can go to hell for all I care. I let you in, Rain! And I've only let one other person in my whole entire life in! My family is falling apart, my social life is nil, and just when I needed you, you decided to bail. So tell me, what the hell is so important you would make me fight through all of this crap scared and alone? I want to hear it, and it better be good!"

Slowly, answering anger began to boil in my veins. I felt heat rush to my face. I looked her dead in the eyes. And I let her see all of the anger and hate I felt, not just directed at her but at everyone who had ever hurt me. I knew it wasn't fair to direct it all at her, but it felt so good to just let go of it all, for once.

"You want to know, Clare? Fine. I'll tell you. Actually, I'll tell you for the second time." My voice was completely calm, and I barely spoke above a whisper. But there was no way she could possibly mistake my demeanor for calm.

"See, the first time I told you was when you were at my house. But the next morning you didn't remember a thing because you had blacked out because you got so drunk. Do you even know how much it hurt the next day when you didn't remember the honest to God most important confession of my life? Pretty damn bad."

She rolled her eyes. "Oh come on. Lay it on me. It can't be that bad. Plus, what do you have to lose? We're done either way, right?"

"You don't understand, do you?" I retorted. "We moved away from Texas for a reason. I'm transgender, Clare. I'm trans, and I cut myself over it. I tried to kill myself over it, and you didn't even have the decency to be sober enough to remember me telling you about it. So there you have it. My guts all out in the open. Happy now?" I did exactly the opposite of Clare and finished in a whisper.

She started to laugh. Huge, cruel laughs. I flinched once. And then I clenched my fists and refused to move. Her eyes crinkled with the force of her laughter, and she actually doubled over, clutching her stomach. I didn't dare move a muscle. When Clare was finally done, she wiped her eyes free of the tears that had formed. And took a moment to compose herself.

"Wow. You honestly think I care about that? You think that would actually bother me? You obviously don't know me as well as I thought you did." With that, she strode off, painting still in hand.

I didn't go after her. I let her take the painting, and with it, I let her take my anger and regrets. I really wasn't in the mood to deal with them right now.

I drove myself home, studied for my test in English, showered, ate, and went straight to bed, where I cried basically all night long.

It was finally starting to dawn on me that I had not only lost, but thrown away, the first real relationship I'd ever had.

I know, I know, first relationships never last. Except we had both been starting to really fall in love with and trust each other. And then I let fear get in my way and cloud my judgment.

And because I was feeling masochistic, I got out of bed sometime in the middle of the night and listened to all of Clare's voice mails. I read her e-mails and her texts, too.

I spent the night staring at her words, first of concern, then hurt, and finally anger. Idly, I wondered if she wasn't sleeping, either. Maybe she had gotten drunk, again. I wondered if someday we would ever be able to fix things. Or, more accurately, if I would ever find a way to mend the rift between us.

I was the only one who needed to do any mending. As far as I knew, anyway.

CLARE TOSSED her keys onto her bed, carelessly. She wrapped her arms tightly around herself, hugging Rain's painting to her chest. The tears rolled freely down her cheeks.

A little part of Clare was relieved that Rain was gone. That she was once again alone with herself, alone with her guilt. She wasn't surprised that things hadn't worked out between them. After all, what right did she have to be happy after that night?

Clare shuddered. She stood slowly and propped the painting against her window. She would rather look at her window and see that than the empty town that would swallow her whole if she let the demons inside her out.

She picked up her phone and dialed Rain's number. She had no right to be mad at Rain anymore. Well, maybe she did, but she didn't want to be. She was too tired from grieving to have the energy it took to be angry anymore. What she wanted desperately at the moment was to tell someone about it. To let someone else help her carry the burden weighing so heavy on her shoulders, dragging her down to hell.

Clare stared at the phone screen a long time, hesitating to complete the call, and thought back to Rain's face when they had parted in the hallway. Her eyes had been completely empty. Like she had been hollowed out, and the only thing left of her was a husk. Clare shivered and tossed the phone away from herself. Being angry might take more energy, but it was also safer for her.

She sat up all night long, staring at the painting in her window, seeing nothing but Rain and the future together that they had both thrown away—even though Clare knew it was herself that she had run from in that hallway, not Rain.

And Rain had no idea what the reason had been for her leaving like that. Sure, Rain being transgender had come as a shock, but it hadn't bothered Clare particularly. Rain was who she was now, and that was all that mattered. And she'd lost Rain.

So Clare spent much of the night crying, trying to shut down but remembering, anyway. Remembering one name over and over again. Remembering one night until she slipped into a waking nightmare that followed her into sleep when she finally dozed off near dawn. Even when she woke up to her alarm clock a bare hour after she'd drifted off to sleep, the nightmare stayed with her. It followed her around the house as she got ready for school. It was freaking haunting her.

To put it lightly, she was losing it, and she felt like Rain wasn't that far behind her. Something bad was coming, and Clare felt it all the way down to her bones.

NINETEEN

I SIGHED, pulling at my shirt. *C'mon, Raimi. You can do this. Just take your Spanish test and don't flunk it. Then you can skip the rest of the day, and you won't have to deal with any of it, anymore.*

I shuffled into class my feet literally dragging a little, I was so reluctant to face her. Thankfully, she wasn't there yet. I sat down and buried my head in my study notes.

Clare came in shortly after I took my seat. We didn't even glance at each other. It was like we were both desperate to avoid one another but hoping we wouldn't be able to. It was pointless, in other words.

Brad didn't come to class. I didn't blame him for skipping. This test was 30 percent of our grade in the class, and the only bigger test we would take this semester was our actual final exam. He would no doubt get the other kids to tell him what was on the test before he made it up.

I shivered the entire class. I had left my big winter coat at home. The weatherman had said we were supposed to be back in the midforties by this morning, but instead, it had yet to hit thirty degrees and was showing no signs of warming up any more.

The lying bastard had also said that it wasn't going to snow, hail, or sleet. And yet there was a constant *plink* against the window that could only be explained by precipitation of some kind. Maybe it was the Clare Effect on the weather. The bottom of the windowsill was dusted with a fine white substance that was either cocaine or snow. I was pretty sure it was snow, though.

The Spanish exam sped by. I conjugated verbs with the best of them and translated like it was second nature. Which it was, by now. I turned my test in with confidence at the end of the period. I actually felt a tiny bit better and ended up staying for the rest of my morning classes.

Everyone was nicer with each other than usual and just in a better mood overall. I thought it was a result of the weather. Everyone seemed to be enjoying the snow. The winter so far had been relatively mild besides that early cold snap we'd had.

I felt a pang in my gut when I thought about how I'd spent that first cold snap. My mind went to the painting, and I sincerely hoped that Clare hadn't used it as kindling.

I walked into the lunchroom like normal, but immediately, I knew something wasn't right. For one thing, everyone was silent. Secondly, the people were dispersed so that there was a huge circle in the middle of the room. Thirdly, there were no staff members anywhere in sight. And lastly, Brad stood in the middle of the circle with his arms crossed. He was staring directly at me.

I stopped just inside the threshold and searched the crowd for familiar faces. Cam and Freddie were nowhere in sight and neither was Clare. Brad stood there, his jaw clenching and unclenching manically. His pupils were seriously dilated, and I honestly thought he might be high on something. That theory only became more likely as the seconds ticked past.

I finally cleared my throat and croaked, "Am I missing something?"

The crowd looked restless. It was only then that I noticed Brad's friends were spread out evenly through the crowd. This was turning more and more into a bad, late-night movie scene.

Brad snorted. "Other than the memo that you're a boy, not much."

I froze. I swear my heart stopped. Someone in the back of the room coughed. No one said a thing. No one moved. It was utter silence.

I laughed nervously. "What are you talking about?"

Brad strode toward me, his jaw stiff. He got right up in my face. His breath smelled weird, like blood cologne. "You know exactly what I'm talking about, you worthless piece of trash tranny." Brad actually spat a little on me because he was speaking with such conviction.

The blood drained from my face. "I have no idea what you—"

He punched me square on the chin. Pain blossomed through my teeth. Brad grabbed me by the front of my shirt and pushed me against the wall.

"I didn't say you could talk, you little shit. Shut up and listen," he growled at me. I tried to nod, but I was so rigid with terror that I couldn't move a muscle.

No one moved. No one spoke. It was like they were all ignoring what was happening, or too captivated to stop it.

"You listen up. I don't know why the hell you came here, but I want you gone. You're a monster, you know that, right? You're the type of thing that little kids have nightmares about. You're unnatural, and you're worthless. You know you're going to hell, right? You're disgusting."

His calm voice was definitely scarier than if he had been screaming and yelling at me. He slammed me back again, and my skull connected sickeningly with the painted walls. My vision was blurred over with tears.

Brad laughed. "You know, I don't hit girls. But it's okay for me to do this."

He let go of me and punched me again, this time in the eye. He kicked me in the stomach, a lot like he had done to Freddie. I fell on the floor. I didn't even register the sound of the cafeteria door opening.

I heard Brad's voice vaguely from somewhere above me. I was in so much pain I had trouble understanding him, though. "She left me for this, everybody. She left the best guy at the school for a stupid, worthless tranny. What a whore. I guess she'll take it wherever she can get it, won't she?"

Brad snickered cruelly. I heard someone crying. I spat blood onto the linoleum floor. He kicked me again, this time in the throat. Spots appeared all over my vision. I didn't even know if there were tears coming out or not. I felt numb. This wasn't real.

No one said a word. No one moved.

"Did you honestly think you could have something with her? I heard you two in the hallway, yesterday. It was pathetic. That whore couldn't even love you. Nothing could love you. You don't even know what love is, do you? You make me sick! You don't deserve to live!" Brad screamed.

I saw his fist come toward me. I closed my eyes. I didn't want to be conscious anymore. I hadn't even really started to understand what was happening. I waited for his fist to connect. And waited. But it didn't come. I opened my eyes.

Clare stood over me. She held Brad's fist in her hands and spoke in a voice that would have carried to every corner of the dead silent cafeteria, "How dare you, Brad. You're a coward and a liar and pathetic. You had to blackmail me to even get near me. You're just jealous that you lost the only girl you ever loved in your own twisted little way to someone who's quite frankly, a better human being than you."

His crazed stare bored into her. He was obviously high on something. What, I didn't know. Clare shoved him back with more force than he was expecting, and he stumbled a few steps. She glared at him a moment longer and then turned on our avid audience.

"You're all sick. You watched him beat a girl up, and no one did a thing. You all talk a big game about doing what's right. But then again, I'm just a worthless gay whore, so what do I know? Go home and tell mommy that the big bad fag told you all to go to hell, today. I'm sure that would make for a great discussion at the dinner table." She laughed bitterly.

"It's a he, not a she! How can you stand to be near that... that thing?" Brad screamed.

Clare rolled her eyes. "Because I love her," she answered matter-of-factly.

A few people gasped. I was one of them, even though it hurt like hell to do so.

"You're a slut, Clare." Brad spat. He slurred his words slightly and was starting to lose his balance.

"Go home, Brad. You're... well, you aren't drunk, but you're definitely high. Have fun in prison. I'm sure you'll be a great bitch," Clare retorted sarcastically.

Had I been more aware of my surroundings, and in a lot less pain, I probably would've laughed uproariously. But I wasn't.

Clare helped me up. I felt like I had been run over by a truck. Someone ran to get a teacher.

A little voice in the rational corner of my mind announced archly that Brad was done for. My mom was a lawyer, and she would have no mercy on anyone who'd assaulted her baby. It actually promised to be quite a show in court when Brad finally got sober enough to plead his case.

Clare led me slowly down a series of familiar hallways. Huh. She had taken me to the art room. The teacher wasn't in, so Clare took down the first aid kit off the wall herself. I lay down on one of the counters, my head spinning so violently I thought I might be sick. I closed my eyes. The last thing I saw for a while was Clare taking my hand very gingerly in hers and squeezing it reassuringly.

WHEN I came to, I was still on the counter. Something soft was under my head, now. Quiet voices were drifting in from the hallway. I recognized Clare's at once. And then the principal's. And there was a third voice I couldn't identify. I blinked blearily at the big clock on the wall over the teacher's desk. I was asking myself if I had really been out for more than fifteen minutes when Clare popped her head back in the room.

She smiled grimly at me as she announced over her shoulder, "She's awake."

The principal, a police officer, and an EMT walked in. The first two asked me a bunch of questions about what had happened while the EMT checked me for concussions and patched me up. What I couldn't answer, Clare filled in for me.

Eventually, I had told them everything I knew and gave them my mom's phone number. My parents were once again out of town with Zach. The fit my mother threw over the phone was audible halfway across the room.

While I was grateful for her mama-bear response, I didn't feel up to dealing with the drama just now and turned down an offer to talk with her. I was tired and I hurt and I just wanted to relax and breathe in the smell of paint and pastels for a while in the art room. As if she knew that without my having to tell her, Clare ushered the adults from the room with a promise that she would stay with me until I got home safely.

She closed the door with a sigh of relief.

I smiled wearily at her.

Comically, she brushed her hand across her brow. I wanted to laugh, but I was too rattled. Clare took a hard look at me and switched the lights off as if she knew how much my head hurt and how painful those bright lights were. She crossed the room with long purposeful strides and wrapped her arms around me in a huge hug.

"I'm so sorry, Rain," she murmured.

I tried to smile, to tell her it wasn't her fault, but opening my mouth made my split lip burn with pain, and I just winced instead. Clare stepped back and started dabbing at my cheeks with something she found in the first aid kit.

"Why do you call me Rain?" I asked gingerly, moving my lips as little as possible. I figured there would never be a better time to ask her.

She kept dabbing at my slow seeping tears, and I looked out the long wall of windows overlooking the football field. Brad had spent countless hours on that field. And now he was going to be charged with several crimes up to and including illegal substance abuse. I tried to picture the little boy who had been Clare's first kiss. For some inexplicable reason, I hoped that boy was still inside him, somewhere.

I shuddered at the thought of how much people could change. Luckily, Clare was there to shake me from those dark thoughts.

"Why do I call you Rain?" she repeated.

I nodded solemnly.

Clare busied herself with taking care of me and held an ice pack to my chin. "Because someone as pretty as you needs an equally pretty name to suit them." Her voice was hushed as snow fell outside the window. I shivered a little at how cold and beautiful it was.

Clare stared straight into my eyes and whispered, "I love you, Raimi."

Hearing her say my name felt foreign, different, and completely right. I reached out and put my hand on her cheek. I smiled, my thumb running along her cheekbone.

"I love you too, Clare."

We just stood there like that for a while. Her holding an ice pack to my wrecked face, my hand resting on her perfect cheek. We didn't move until someone finally knocked on the door to check on us again. Nervously. My mom must have really put the fear of God into the principal.

"Just take me home," I mumbled.

"You got it." She put her arm around my shoulder, and I looped mine around her waist.

When we got to the parking lot, she turned to me. "Whose car is comfier, yours or mine?"

I thought for a moment. "Neither. The comfiest car on the planet is my mom's SUV."

"We'll take my car, then. We're going back to your house. I'm going to call your mom and convince her to let us go on a little road trip, and you aren't going to ask any questions," Clare said sternly.

I raised my eyebrows at her. "Okay, then…." I said wryly.

Her giggle made my heart squeeze.

There was a really big part of me that just wanted to break down, cry, and remember the awfulness that had just happened to me. But there was another part of me that wanted to dive into wherever Clare was going to take us. I didn't want to know where we were going, how we were going to get there, or how long it would take to get there. I just wanted to leave with Clare. I wanted to be with her and let go of reality for a little while.

So I did.

TWENTY

I STUDIED Clare suspiciously. What the heck was she up to?

She met my look evenly. "Give me the phone, Rain. You know you want to. Just hand it over, and this won't hurt a bit."

I snorted skeptically.

"We can either do this the easy way or the hard way," she teased. "Really, it's up to you. But I *am* going to end up with that phone in my hand."

She was a cheerleader, after all, and could throw girls my size fifteen feet over her head and catch them on the way back down. I laughed and handed over my phone as she closed the front door of my parents' house behind her. She pressed the green call button, and we waited anxiously for my mom to pick up. Clare put a finger to her mouth to hush me and started speaking,

"Hi, Mrs. Carter, it's Clare. Yes, I'm with her now, and she's fine. Well, not fine, but she'll live."

She paused to listen for a minute. "Of course, I'll tell her." Then as promised, Clare said to my mom, "I need to talk with you for a minute. I wanted to run an idea by you." She started to back away from me. I tried to follow, but she waved me back as she ducked into my dad's study.

I threw my hands up impatiently, and she blew me a silent kiss through the doorway. I sighed, pushing away the hair that had fallen in my face as Clare closed the door to my dad's study behind her. *What da heck?*

I desperately fought an urge to eavesdrop. It helped, though, that I felt like crap. I ended up lying down on the living room sofa to await the verdict from my mom.

Clare finally emerged from the office and smiled at me brightly. "It was a hard sell, but she bought my plan. Pack anything you need for a five-day road trip. Maybe six. Depending on how you feel. Your mom made me promise not to push you too hard." She winked, her words bright and excited.

"A five-day *what?*" I exclaimed.

Her laughter tinkled through the air musically. "A five-day road trip, honey. Are you telling me you've never experienced the grueling automobile trek of our people?"

I shook my head gingerly. I thought she was going to smack me in her shock.

"Well, we'll just have to fix that now, won't we?" she scolded.

I smiled tiredly, and she twirled a piece of my hair between her fingers. "C'mon. Let's go pack."

She kissed me on the forehead and then led me toward the stairs. It felt really nice to be taken care of like this. So often, I was the one caring for the people I loved and not the other way around.

TWO HOURS later, we were both packed. Luckily, I had some clothes that both fit her body *and* her taste. It had been a struggle, though, believe me.

Clare surveyed our handiwork carefully. "I think we might be ready to go."

I nodded. We could live out of these bags for easily double our estimated trip time, but one can never be too prepared. And plus, it wasn't like my mom's huge SUV was going to run out of room anytime soon. I couldn't believe Clare had talked my mom into letting us take her car for our trip.

Clare beamed at me as we hauled our stuff down the stairs. "I would suggest we get any last minute restroom stops out of the way now. We have almost two thousand miles to cover in the next two days if the Internet is correct."

I about fell over. "Two thousand miles?" I squeaked incredulously.

She nodded and shot me a look that said she had no idea what the big deal was. "I'll drive. You can sleep the whole time."

I started to pinch the bridge of my nose but stopped as my fingers encountered a bandage and tender flesh. This relationship would seriously never cease to amaze me. I highly doubted Clare would ever be low maintenance. At all. Ever. And that was one of the things I loved most about her.

WE BRAKED to a stop in front of Clare's house. I squeezed her hand, and she took a deep breath before she opened the driver's side door. She told me that her dad wasn't supposed to be home until a lot later, and that her mom was usually passed out by now. I sincerely hoped she was right. I waited nervously for her to return, blasting the heat, and fiddling with the car's radio to distract myself.

When she emerged from her house, I was glad to see a tentative smile plastered over her face. The closer she got to the SUV, the more her shoulders relaxed back into her normal posture.

So of course, right as she climbed in, her dad's car just had to turn onto this street. I ducked down beneath the dash, and she immediately peeled away from the curb. I didn't need her dad glaring at me with hatred in his eyes. I'd had enough of being hated on for one day.

He must not have seen Clare because he didn't follow us or send the police after us. That was all that mattered to me at that point. When our SUV had finally merged safely onto the freeway, Clare let out a breath I hadn't known she was holding.

"We did it. We did it," she whispered to herself.

I giggled nervously. "Of course, we did."

She nodded absentmindedly, withdrawn almost, changing the setting on the radio that I had dialed in not ten minutes before.

I sighed. "Is my taste in music really that bad?"

Clare looked over at me blankly, blinking a few times like she was just now waking up from a dream. I alternated between looking at the road and trying to decipher what was going on in her mind.

Maybe fifteen minutes passed before I tried talking with her again. I kept my eyes on the highway this time, though. I figured if I gave her some space, it would be easier for her to open up and talk about whatever had happened in her house just now. Because something had definitely changed from when she went in to when she came out of that hellhole.

"What did you tell your mom?" I said flatly. I winced. My voice had not been what I wanted it to be. "Sorry that sounded rude," I added hastily. "I just meant, what happened? You did a complete one-eighty personality flip in under five minutes."

"Nothing happened, surprisingly. Mom was passed out on the couch instead of her bed, but that was the only noticeable thing out of the ordinary. I just went in, grabbed my toothbrush and credit card, and left."

Clare's voice was emotionless and impossible to get a read on. My brow creased in confusion. I didn't get a chance to ask her any more questions. She got busy navigating lane changes and exits as we approached the urban sprawl of New York City. It was peaceful just being in the car with her like this. But it also felt empty, like something was missing.

One thing stuck out to me, though. Clare had flinched and her face paled the minute it starting snowing. Eventually, the snow turned into a sad slush-like substance that wasn't quite sleet, wasn't quite snow, and definitely wasn't hail.

Something was wrong with Clare. And the only thing I could hope to do was be there for her if and when she ever wanted to talk about it with me. I prayed that time was coming soon. I was tired of barriers and secrets between us.

TWENTY-ONE

WE PULLED in at a ratty-looking motel around ten o'clock that night after driving for a little under six hours. To say I was exhausted wouldn't quite cover it. Clare paid quietly for our room with her credit card. I eyed her carefully.

"Are you sure you're allowed to be using that thing?" I said incredulously. She gave me a little half laugh.

"Daddy gave it to me on my sixteenth birthday. Brad and I had been together for a year, and this was my reward for—I don't know, not screwing up my relationship as badly as my dad did. Anyway, there's no way he would cut me off from this thing. It's one of the only reminders he has left from my days in the oh-so-wonderful closet."

I shook my head. Family dynamics are interesting little things.

With that lovely thought swirling around in my mind, Clare and I trudged up two flights of stairs to our room. Let me stress how out of date this motel was. It didn't have an elevator, even though it had like six floors. The logic behind that actually had me giggling moronically as Clare and I unlocked our room. Clare didn't say a word, just sprawled herself over one of the beds and ordered room service. I was asleep on my own bed before the food even got there.

That's how tired I was. Food couldn't even motivate me to stay awake.

I WOKE up around ten the next morning. I shuffled blearily into the bathroom, stumbling over our suitcases in the process. I let my head loll back in the shower, rubbing my neck to try to get some of the knots out. Steam rose around me lazily as the water pounded out some of my soreness left over from Brad's fists. I reached out a hand and traced one of the opaque tendrils. I started to worry about Clare and immediately decided it would be better to just not think at all. It was easier, at least.

When I finished my shower, I dressed and went back out into the room. Clare had turned on the TV and ordered pancakes and waffles while I was showering. She smiled bleakly up at me.

"A few messages came through on your phone," Clare said cautiously.

I nodded, picking my phone up gingerly. They were all from Brad. I snorted and deleted all of them. I couldn't remember the last time I actually opened anything from him.

Clare rose silently and grabbed a pile of clothes. She closed the bathroom door behind her quietly. When I heard the click, I relaxed tension in my shoulders I didn't know I had been holding.

My spidey senses were tingling over Clare. I could almost see the walls she was putting up around her. The thought of it made me nauseous. I ate my breakfast in silence, the drone of a local news station filling my ears. I let myself drown in the emptiness, letting go of everything else for now. Sometimes being numb is a nice change of pace. I put on a little makeup to cover my blossoming bruises and pass the time. The minutes slipped by like quicksand, and without meaning.

EVENTUALLY, CLARE emerged from her shower, steam rolling along the carpet when she opened the door. She picked up her things without speaking and left the room. I hurried after her, not bothering to turn off the TV. We drove quietly, only stopping to grab food and then keep going. I felt good enough to take a few turns at driving so Clare could take naps. My mom called every other hour like clockwork to check on us, but other than those calls, we were mostly silent.

We spent that night at a slightly nicer motel. The ice cream bar in the lobby was a divine gift, and after eating our body weight in frozen yogurt, we turned in late.

When we woke up, Clare and I took our time getting ready, not rushing anything. We only had about a six-hour drive left to our final destination, and Clare said we could only do what she had planned after 4:00 p.m.

I speculated endlessly over the possibility of what it could be. The first time Clare's face had lit up in forty-eight hours was when I tried to guess, to no avail, where we were headed.

"Is it... a monkey?" I teased.

Clare laughed genuinely. "Yes, Rain, I totally got you a monkey. Guess again." She rolled her eyes, and I grinned despite myself.

"Are we going to a zoo?" I guessed. She shook her head again. I sighed. And then a sign came into view. I started to laugh.

"We're in Colorado. We're in freaking Colorado!" I threw my head back and just laughed, even though that probably wasn't the smartest thing to do when you're driving along a major highway. Clare broke out into a huge smile and beamed at me.

I hummed softly to myself until she broke into my melody. "Here's your interesting yet trivial fact for the day, Rain. Colorado has no restrictions on minors getting tattoos."

I about lost control of the car. "Oh. My. God," I whispered.

Clare snickered. "I think the words you're looking for are 'thank' and 'you.'"

I shook my head, completely taken aback. "Life is never dull with you, is it?"

Her smile grew even bigger. "Nope."

146

TWENTY-TWO

WE PULLED into the tattoo parlor parking lot, and I felt my stomach sinking and my heart rising into my throat. I'm pretty sure I started hyperventilating.

Clare just grinned at me. "Are you telling me you've never wanted a tattoo? What are you, a nun?"

I gave a short bark of nervous laughter. She reached across the SUV as I parked it carefully. She took my hand in hers and squeezed firmly.

"Everything is going to be just fine," she leaned over to whisper in my ear, her breath tickling my neck. I blushed furiously. No matter how long I was around her, no matter how many times she kissed me, she always had a way of making me shiver. I hoped that would never go away.

My phone buzzed, and I ignored it. Clare bit her lip and smiled playfully at me. "You should get that."

Her lips met mine and everything felt normal again. In an adrenaline kind of way. Her free hand knotted in my hair, and my free hand found her neck. It was awkward kissing over the console, but we made it work. Just when I thought the moment was absolutely perfect, voices met our ears.

We turned to look out the fogging windshield and saw a group of three boys. They were whistling and catcalling at us. Clare's face flushed with anger, her hand falling from my hair and clenching into a fist.

I looked at the boys and back at her again. Then I leaned over and kissed her again. She was stiff and surprised, but eventually she relaxed. I let my hair fall in front of me so that the boys couldn't see my lips move tenderly against hers.

"Don't let them get to you. They're just jealous because you're so hot."

She snorted. "You don't give yourself enough credit. Still, I don't want to let them see us. It feels wrong," she explained.

I shook my head and kissed the spot just below her ear, murmuring, "Love is love, Clare. And love is never wrong."

When we got out of the car, I immediately took her hand, apprehension already choking my throat. I felt my heart stutter in my chest like a bird taking its first flight. Clare clung to my side, reassuring me the entire way. The boys were still watching us, but that wasn't high on either of our priority lists at the moment.

The tattoo parlor looked like any ordinary tattoo place from the outside. Clare opened the door for me and ushered me in. The floor was a plush white shag carpet I might've expected to see in the sixties—or maybe in my dad's man cave. There was a tiny waiting room with plastic chairs and a scarred coffee table littered with books of tattoo designs.

The walls were adorned with everything from anime posters to a painted canvas of a lake surrounded by mountains. Instead of a counter, there was a giant fish tank with a cash register resting casually on top of it. Clare breathed in the heavy incense smell and pretended to get high from it.

I giggled shakily. "It's a little retro for my taste, but I like it." My voice cracked at the end, and I blushed an even deeper hue of red.

Clare sneaked a peek at me, and we both laughed. Together, we started undoing our heavy winter coats. It was starting to rain outside,

148

little ice pellets bounding off of the asphalt. It was surreal. Just then, a beautiful woman walked in.

Her hair was black as night and tightly French braided back. Her eyes were like cold fire, the purest blue you could imagine. But where Clare's were a green-blue-turquoise, this woman's were violet-blue like fine sapphires. Her lips were full and pink, and she had on cat-eye makeup. I was jealous that she could wear so much makeup and not look like a raccoon slut. She was maybe five foot eight, but it was hard to tell because she had on stiletto boots a lot like Clare did. Actually, she was wearing something very close to what Clare would wear.

Clare dropped my hand and stood up. "Hey there, Rose. It's great to see you."

Rose just looked at her, tapping her fingers on the top of the fish tank. "Hey there, Clare. It's... it's good to see you, too." Rose paused, like she wasn't quite sure how she felt about us.

Clare motioned at me and said, "This is Raimi, my girlfriend."

I blushed. It was still weird hearing Clare say "girlfriend." The word sounded almost foreign to me. Nevertheless, I tilted my lips up in a polite smile and stood.

"It's nice to meet you, Rose. How do you know Clare?" I asked.

Clare and Rose shared a look before Rose spoke.

"I know her from way back. I was two years ahead of her in school." Rose chose her words carefully, testing each one out in her mouth before continuing.

I nodded cautiously. There was something Clare didn't want me to know. And I had a theory it had to do with why she was so depressed for most of our trip so far. Now I could add Rose to the unspoken mystery. I just wished Clare would tell me and get it over with.

I shook myself out of my speculations when Rose led us into the back. She and Clare exchanged pleasantries as we walked down a long hallway. Clare had always been good at making small talk with anyone, whereas that was not my strong point. At all.

Rose finally motioned us to stop, and she opened an oak door. The room inside was painted black with a painted tile floor. The walls were beautiful, hand-drawn silver filigree decorating every available inch. The ceiling was the only plain thing in the room, a clean, sleek white. There were fluorescent lights tucked away throughout the entire room so that there was light, but you couldn't tell where it was coming from. In the center of the room was a table a lot like you might see in a massage parlor and a chair I recognized from a movie about tattoos.

Absolutely nothing was out of the ordinary in this room. And yet it still felt like there was something I wasn't seeing, a hidden layer just beyond my reach of sight. I brushed the thought off. Maybe it was just the tension that was obvious between Rose and Clare.

Rose pulled several thick books from a short bookshelf and started flipping through pages.

"Do you girls know what you want?" she inquired. I shook my head. Clare nodded slowly, like she wasn't sure of it herself until that moment.

Rose raised an eyebrow. "Clare, you want to go first?"

Clare laughed nervously and waved her off. "Nah, I'm good with going second."

Rose rolled her eyes. "Whatever floats your boat." Her voice was flat. She turned her gaze on me. "What about you, Rain, is it?" she asked.

"Yeah, you can call me Rain," I beamed. She passed me a book, and I flipped through the pages.

In my head, I went back through all of the tattoos I had seen on people over the years. I knew I didn't want an animal or skulls or guns. I decided against a flower as I looked through the book. I thought about what a tattoo should mean.

It should say something about you, considering it's permanent. It has to be something that's going to be in you for the rest of your life not just a whim. I closed my eyes and flipped to a random page. I smiled when I saw it and knew that it was perfect. I pointed it out to Rose.

She smiled at me and said, "That's one of my favorites. Where do you want it?"

I thought about it for a minute. "Right shoulder blade," I said firmly. That way it wasn't something for me to look at. It was something for other people to see on me. Plus, it would be a good way to sass people if I ever needed to storm out and make a truly spectacular exit.

I took my shirt off and slid my bra strap to the side so Rose could begin. She laid me down on the massage table. I felt her hands gently, but confidently preparing my skin. Clare glanced at what I had picked and just beamed at me.

I closed my eyes, content. The sting of the needle was as much a relief as it was painful. This tattoo was what I needed. It truly proved I was out of the closet. I was done hiding that I was gay. I was done hiding that I was trans.

I was finally me. Not the labels anyone put on me. I was free to be whomever I wanted.

When Rose was finished, she put up a mirror so I could see the reflection. I thought my cheeks would burst from smiling so big. It was exactly what I wanted.

The word Free was spelled out in the trademark rainbow of gay pride. The script was outlined in black, making it stand out against my skin. The letters were beautiful, the font not big enough to look garish, but not so small that you couldn't see it. Clare whistled.

"Nice job, Rose. That's gorgeous," Clare said reverently.

Rose snorted in response. "Of course it is. I don't suck at this, you know."

I commented dryly, "Just as a rule of thumb, Clare, never piss off a tattoo artist right before they tattoo you."

Rose laughed warmly. "You should listen to your girlfriend more often." Rose snuck me a wink.

Clare sighed heavily, exasperated with us. "Do you know what you want, drama queen?" Rose sounded like she could be Clare's older sister.

My brow furrowed. That thought had occurred offhandedly, but I actually took a minute to think about it. The fit would be perfect, except I knew Clare was an only child. The familiarity between them was startling, though. I filed away my thoughts on the subject for now.

Clare tapped her chin thoughtfully, obviously drawing the process out for effect. And then she started stripping. She scooted me off of the table and unzipped her jeans. I nearly squeaked. If she was getting a tramp stamp, I thought I was going to just go ahead and end the relationship then and there. But instead, she lay on her back and tugged her pants down and her shirt up. Her fingers traced the line of skin in between her hipbones.

"I want it to read 'Everyone gets wet in the rain,'" she murmured. I had to stifle a giggle.

"You want the word wet right there?" Rose raised an eyebrow, and her voice was stunned.

Clare face-palmed and laughed lightly. "Would you two please get your minds out of the gutter for like, two seconds? Yes, I want exactly what I said, exactly where I pointed," she declared sternly.

Rose threw her hands up in defeat, but she was still smiling brightly. "Do you want anything on the ends?" she asked.

But Clare had already closed her eyes and just mumbled, "Mmm hmm."

I watched with curiosity as Rose prepared Clare's skin like she had mine. Once Rose began the actual tattooing, it was fascinating to watch unfold. She was completely in the zone, her eyes fixed intently on Clare's skin. It was almost like watching them both enter a trance. About halfway through, tears leaked down Clare's cheeks. I didn't say anything. The tattooing had been pretty painful, but I didn't think it was enough to bring Clare to tears.

Confused, I took her hand and squeezed it. For a minute, it felt like she was going to let go of me. But instead, her fingers laced through mine familiarly.

ROSE ENDED up putting something on the ends—a rose, filigree, and a Celtic knot on both of Clare's hipbones. Again, her tattoo was absolutely beautiful. Clare silently dressed, wiping away the little bit of makeup that had smudged from her crying.

I looped my arm around her waist when she was done and hugged her gently. She returned the gesture, her hands gingerly pressed against the middle of my back. We relaxed against each other for a moment before Rose cleared her throat and we stepped apart.

Rose took us back to the cash register and rang us up. Clare didn't even let me see how much it had cost.

I shook my head, thanking Clare quietly. I went out to the car to get the heater started, and Clare lagged back in the store. I pulled up at the curb in front of the tattoo place and waited for her to come out. I squinted through the window and told myself not to get jealous as I saw them embrace. No, I wasn't going to get jealous. They were probably like sisters back when she and Rose went to school together.

At least that's what I told myself as Clare climbed back into the SUV. She winced a little as she buckled her seatbelt, the strap cutting right across where her tattoo was. I let my lips tilt up when she glanced over at me. And I pretended to ignore the fact that her eyes were somehow completely empty and overflowing with emotion.

TWENTY-THREE

WE DROVE silently as far as we could that night before crashing at another motel and eating cheap Chinese food. Clare had nightmares all night long. I heard her tossing and turning the entire time. I shuddered, thinking about what kind of demons she had to be facing to be that scared. I barely slept.

The next day was almost exactly the same. Clare remained silent unless it was to give directions. Only the weather differed from the other days of endless driving. It snowed the entire day, building from flurries that were pleasant and lazy to a blizzard with howling winds.

Clare seemed to grow more and more anxious as the minutes ticked by, like she was standing on ice and she could feel it cracking out from under her. I was really starting to worry about her.

I pulled into our next motel stop early, the clock on the dash showing it to be just seven at night. Clare was too dazed to notice that we had stopped until I tapped her. Sluggishly, she turned to look at me. I gave her a supportive smile, not entirely sure what she needed. The only thing I knew how to do was be with her. So that's what I did.

THE POWER went out at around three in the morning. Clare nudged me awake. She slipped into my bed, her feet freezing.

I squeaked a little. "Oh my God. Your toes are like ice cubes!" I gasped.

She let out a poor imitation of her real laugh. My gut wrenched just hearing it. I shivered but not from the cold. I sat up in bed, and unable to see what was going on outside, I ventured over to the window, peeking past the curtains. I sucked in a chilled breath, the cold air dry against the back of my throat.

"Clare, come here! I swear there's gotta be at least a foot of snow covering everything."

"You have to remember, Rain, I grew up in the north, where snow is a common thing. If you wanted to impress me, you'd show me three feet of snow. Now that would be gasp-worthy."

I rolled my eyes, even though she couldn't see them. It was quiet in the room. Finally, I snapped. I couldn't take it anymore. I needed to know what was going on, and I needed to know right then.

I whirled away from the window and met her blue eyes as fiercely as I could. But before I could say a word, she started talking.

"I know you're upset with me for not telling you what's been going on. But you have to understand, I've only ever told one person, and that backfired pretty bad."

I nodded, listening hard.

"But it's time I told you the story behind the picture Brad had." Clare's voice was even and patient. I sat down as her words started to fill the air around me.

"Do you remember the story I told you about my first kiss? Well, there's more to it than that. My *real* first kiss was Andrea. Kissing her was the moment, the night, when I realized I was gay. I mean, I had never felt all that attracted to a guy before. But when I kissed her, I felt alive. Like I was finally doing something right."

I knew the feeling. It had been exactly that way when I kissed her.

She continued. "To say I freaked would be an understatement. I didn't speak to anyone for a week afterward. I pretended I was sick so my dad wouldn't make me go to school. I read the Bible around the clock, praying to God that I wasn't gay. Eventually, it was Brad who got me to go back to school. Brad was one of my closest friends at that point, and I had no idea he had a crush on me."

"When I went back to school, Andrea would come up and talk to me in the hall. I avoided her as much as possible. Every time I was near her, I got butterflies in my stomach. I was in complete denial at that point and would throw myself at any guy who wanted me at a party to prove that I was straight. I even made out with Brad one night to prove to everyone else that I was straight, too."

Clare had to take a minute before she kept speaking. She took in a wracking breath, her teeth chattering like she was cold. She pulled the comforter tighter around her before she continued.

"I was in a dark place. When I started cutting myself, that's when Andrea stepped in." Clare smiled despite herself the more she spoke.

"She finally came up to me one day at school and asked what the hell was going on. I almost lost it in front of everyone. But she was in the closet too, so no one suspected anything. She gave me her phone number and said that if I ever wanted to talk to her, or just to someone, to give her a call. And one day, I did. She took me out to dinner, and we got to talking.

"The more time I spent with her, the more I wanted to know her. I wanted to listen to her talk, I wanted to hear what she had to say, and more importantly, I wanted her to feel the same way. It was so easy to fall for her without even realizing it. We eventually exchanged 'I love yous,' and from there, we didn't look back."

Clare met my eyes briefly before her gaze flickered away. Her words grew quieter and quieter until she was speaking only barely above a whisper.

"It was the middle of winter, and I was over at her house. We had been together for almost eight months, even though no one knew about us. She and I were talking about coming out of the closet together. Andrea was ready to tell people about being gay, but I wasn't. She didn't understand my reluctance. We took a drive together and ended up at my house. My parents weren't home, and things heated up between us. Long story short, we ended up making out. We were so focused on each other neither of us heard the door open.

"That's where Brad came in. He saw us together before we heard him. I flipped total shit and kicked him out of my house. Andrea didn't even care. She was ready for everyone to know and had nothing to lose. Unlike mine, her parents didn't care. We fought again, and I ended it. I said that she should feel free to come out, but that I wasn't going to follow her. So she left."

Clare stopped, choking back tears. Part of me was screaming to tell her it was okay, that she didn't have to finish. But I knew she did, if not for me, for her.

"I called her about an hour after she left. I loved her, and after thinking about it, I had decided that being afraid of everyone else shouldn't keep me from loving her. When she didn't pick up, I assumed it was because she was mad at me."

Claire took one last, wobbly breath and then plunged ahead. "What I didn't know was that she had driven off a bridge. They think her car took the turn wrong and it fishtailed because of the ice. It had been snowing out, so it would've been really hard for her to see any ice on the road."

Ohmigod. So much made sense to me, now.

Clare swiped at the tears running down her cheeks before she resumed talking. The rhythm of her words sounded rusty and unsure, like she didn't know what came next until she said it.

"When I saw it on the news the next morning, I called Brad, hysterical. I convinced him to come over. I told him everything about Andrea from our first kiss to her leaving and crashing her car. He was sympathetic. God, he held me! That's when he showed me the picture he had. He said he would make a deal with me. Except it wasn't a deal, it was blackmail. He told me that no one had to see it if I did exactly as he said."

I had never hated Brad more than I did in that moment. The bastard had taken advantage of her when she was at her most vulnerable, grieving and in pain. What. A. Douche.

Claire continued painfully, "I was tired, I was distraught, and I was on the verge of a very deep depression. And I was desperate to stay in the closet. I had only been willing to come out if Andrea was with me when we did it. I wasn't about to do that alone. So I agreed to his 'deal' and spent years in a living hell."

I realized with some surprise that my own cheeks were wet.

"The reason I brought you out here to Colorado wasn't just to get tattoos and escape for a little while. I knew that making this trip would force me to tell you, because Rose is Andrea's big sister. I knew—well, at least I hoped—that seeing her would give me the strength it would take to tell you."

When Clare finished, I closed the gap between us. I didn't tell her I was sorry for what happened. Because I knew that everything that had happened in her life before had led up to her meeting me. I was sorry that Andrea had to die, but I would never ever be sorry for whatever it took for Clare to find me.

And I didn't let go of her, either.

TWENTY-FOUR

THE SUV finally lumbered into my driveway late the next night. The moon was obscured behind yet another line of approaching snow clouds. I breathed in the chilly night air. I had already dropped Clare off at her house after she assured me she was safe to go home and that she was okay. I parked the SUV in the garage, sliding stiffly from the front seat.

I left everything in the car, eager to just get inside. I toyed with my lips, the brush of her kiss still lingering on my mouth. A blush rose to my cheeks as thoughts of last night drifted lazily through my mind. Life was perfect. When I stepped through my back door, the house was exceptionally cold. I shivered but shrugged off my sweater nonetheless.

My head was in the clouds when I walked into the kitchen. There was a note taped to my kitchen counter. Curious, I picked it up.

> *Dear Raimi,*
>
> *Your father and I took Zach to see my parents. Check your messages for updates on the trial. I love you, sweetheart, and I can't wait to see your new tattoo!*
>
> *Love,*
>
> *Mom*

Sometimes I wondered if my mom blamed herself for my being trans. She talked now and then about not spending enough time with me when I was little. I guess she was trying to make up for her mistakes with me by spending more time with Zach. Of course, my being trans had nothing to do with her. It was just the way I was born, and frankly, I was damned lucky she'd supported my transition.

The note crumpled as my fingers clutched into a fist. *What was this about a trial?* I reread the message several times, trying to understand what she had meant. I pulled out my phone to call her, but it was dead. Sighing, I plugged it in and went to watch some TV.

When I heard a knock at the door, I didn't even think about it. I didn't take into consideration that it was nearly one in the morning, and I didn't think about what the word trial could even mean in reference to me. So I opened the door and found Brad standing there.

His eyes were maniacal and bloodshot. His pupils were familiarly dilated. When he smiled at me, there was blood running down his teeth from his gums. I didn't even have time to scream as I leaped back from him. He raised a handgun and shot.

TWENTY-FIVE

I STUMBLED and fell, the force of the bullet knocking me back. I clutched at my leg, blood starting to warm my fingers. Brad's hand shook as he raised the gun to his mouth.

"No!" I screamed.

But he was too stoned or too lost inside his madness to hear me. I clenched my eyes shut as he pulled the trigger, ending his own life. He might have failed to end mine successfully, but he did not fail to end his. I shook with tears, still holding my leg. I crawled into the kitchen, trying to keep pressure on my leg. I scrabbled to the phone and dialed 911.

"Nine-one-one, what's your emergency?" a woman said pleasantly into the phone.

"I... I got shot in the leg," I stuttered, the adrenaline coursing through my body making it hard to speak.

"Is the shooter still there?" she asked tersely.

Without warning, I started sobbing. "N-no, he killed him-himself," I wailed.

Dizziness pulled at the edge of my vision. The woman spoke in my ear, but I couldn't hear her. All I could hear was the pounding in my ears. All I could see was the corpse lying in my front hallway.

An ambulance picked me up after what felt like years. The EMTs worked over me calmly as they loaded me into the back of the

161

ambulance. I remember shivering and thanking them. But other than that, all of it was a salty, blood-colored blur.

Except for the smell. I will never forget what Brad's blood smelled like, mixed with the gunpowder. Those are the things that stay with you.

TWENTY-SIX

FLORESCENT LIGHTS registered. Flickering, florescent lights. Those and scratchy sheets. My skin felt dry, and my toes itched. My fingers were numb, my first attempts at wiggling them getting me nowhere. A soft beeping sounded in my ear. There was an IV attached to the back of one of my hands.

I started to look beyond the ceiling and the bad lighting. White walls with purple trim. I sat up slowly in my hospital bed. As the blood returned to my hands, I felt someone holding one of them. I glanced to my left. Like déjà vu, my mom was there with coffee in her free hand.

"Hey, sweetie. How are you feeling?" she murmured.

I smiled. She still carried lingering traces of a Spanish accent after visiting her parents. It was a familiar thing among the strangeness around me. I thought about her question. Whatever they were putting in my IV was taking the pain away from my leg. Physically, I was fine. But as the events that had brought me here began flooding through my mind, I was anything but fine. I was scared. I was worried. I was confused. And honestly, I was traumatized.

That's not what my mom needed to hear, though.

"I'm fine. Can't feel a thing," I said confidently, if a little slurred.

She smiled sympathetically at me. "That's good. The last effects of the anesthesia should wear off pretty soon. The doctors wanted to make sure that you would be under long enough to give them time to do anything necessary."

I nodded. Tears pricked the back of my eyes. I could see his body, bloody and mangled where his face used to be, all over again. A little part of me wished I had kept my eyes open to watch him pull the trigger. The success of his suicide was sickly fascinating to me.

"Why did Brad kill himself?" I whispered. I wanted to be a child again. I wanted my mom to scoop me up in her arms and hold me tight until everything felt better.

Instead, I got a squeeze of the hand before she started to explain. I couldn't meet her eyes as she did, so I stared at the ceiling again. It was safer than watching her lips move and tell the story of how someone died.

"He was high. On what, we don't know. As you know, he was facing charges on several different counts. The police wouldn't tell me the details, but somehow, he got possession of the gun and the drugs. They think he was trying to get back at Clare by killing you."

I laughed hollowly. "Well, he didn't do a very good job of it, did he?"

"Raimi! He might've been an awful person, but a death is a death."

I nodded. I heard what she was saying. I agreed with it. I just didn't want to deal with it. I was too tired. Without letting go of her hand, I drifted off into sleep. I was thankful for the reprieve.

I SLEPT for upward of three days, only waking when the occasional nurse appeared. Each time I woke up, there was a new bouquet. I asked the nurse who had sent them.

"From your friends at school," she answered. It was obvious she was surprised I wouldn't have known. I was too tired to question her any further. So instead, I just went back to sleep.

It was on the fourth day when Clare was finally allowed to see me. Our faces lit up when we saw one another. She was the person I had been waiting to come visit me.

"I've missed you, Rain," Clare murmured tenderly, her arms wrapping around me for a light hug.

Her actions suggested she was convinced I would break at any moment, and she might have to glue me back together. Her smile didn't reach far enough into her eyes to chase away the worry there.

I ran my thumb over her palm and whispered, "I've missed you too, Clare."

She kissed me softly. I breathed in deeply, holding her close. "Are you okay?" I murmured. I watched as she pulled back and bit her lip to keep it from trembling.

"Yeah. I'm fine."

I nodded sympathetically at her. "I get it."

Clare nodded. We were quiet for a minute, taking each other in.

Then she murmured, "The weirdest part of this whole situation is how everyone at school has reacted. Brad might actually be the best thing that ever happened to the two of us. When the other kids heard that he shot you, this major outpouring of support happened."

"Really?" I asked in wonder.

Claire nodded. "Brad would hate it. Everyone treats me like royalty. A lot of girls who got blackmailed by him have come out of the woodwork to tell me what happened to them. It'll be interesting to see who goes to his funeral."

I didn't say anything. I had thought about that already. I didn't think there was any reason for me to go except if Clare went. And it didn't sound like she had plans to attend.

A bird sang softly outside my window. Clare walked across the room and closed the door. She took something out of her pocket and smoothed it gently. It looked like a paper napkin. But it obviously meant a lot to Clare. She started reading.

"*Dear Clare,*

I'm sorry I put you through three years of torture. Nothing on earth gave me the right to do the things I did to you, or to anyone. There's a little part of me that will always love you. I've loved you since we met sixteen years ago. You were the only girl I ever really loved. And I put you through hell.

I want to say the only reason I ever went near drugs, or drugged girls, was because of my brother. But that would be a lie. I did it because it made me feel powerful. I did it because it made me feel in control and safe, because girls were easy to dominate.

Here's the truth, though. I kept you from coming out because you really were the only girl I ever loved. I kept you from coming out because I was jealous that you had the strength to do it. And the reason I'm taking a gun to Raimi's house is because maybe, if I do this, it will make up for everything wrong I did to you.

If I hurt Raimi, I know you'll hate me forever. But I'm doing it because I love you and because everyone else will see you two more clearly then. They'll see you two as survivors, as victims, instead of evil, or as lesbians. You always said I had a clever brain and that I should just use it for good. Now, I finally am.

I want to give you one last secret. Killing myself is going to be the only protection I could ever give you. I'm doing this—"

Clare had to stop reading because she was crying too hard to continue. I tugged the napkin from her hand and read the rest aloud.

I'm doing this because I'm gay, too. I'm gay. It's nice to finally say it. I'm sorry that I kept you in the closet with me for all those years.

But maybe now we can all be free."

I looked up at Clare in shock as tears spilled out of my eyes. She just stared back at me, tears of her own running silently down her beautiful face.

We cried together for him, for the poor trapped soul he'd been. And we cried for ourselves and the pain he'd caused us. And then, finally, as we both ran out of tears to shed, we cried in love and gratitude that we were alive. And together. And free.

WINTER PAGE is a freshman in high school. Born and raised in Texas, she has been an athlete her entire life—a figure skater, gymnast, competitive cheerleader, and belly dancer. She started writing after an injury forced her to stop sports. Her goal each year is to write something that makes her English teacher cry. She likes to listen to music, spend time with her friends, and of course, work on her latest novel.

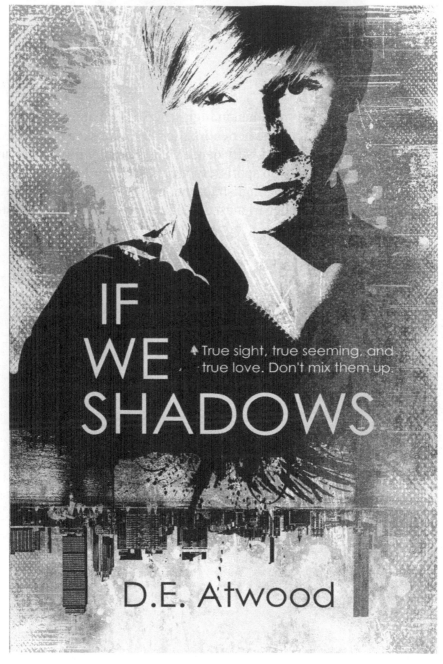

GENE GANT

LESSONS ON
DESTROYING
THE WORLD

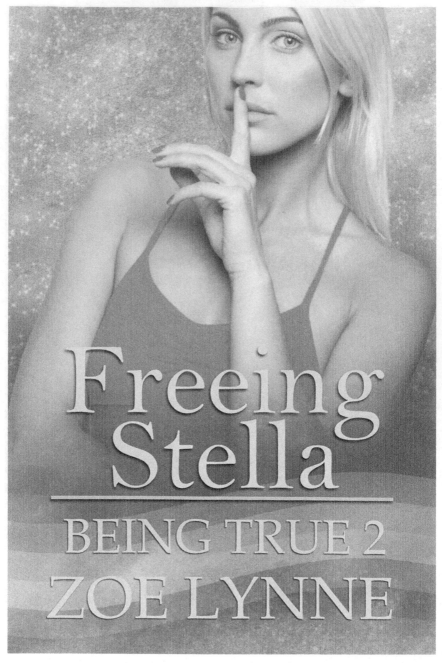

The Other Me

Suzanne van Rooyen

http://www.harmonyinkpress.com

Also from HARMONY INK PRESS

THE RED SHEET

MIA KERICK

http://www.harmonyinkpress.com

Harmony Ink

CPSIA information can be obtained at www.ICGtesting.com
Printed in the USA
BVOW08s1555200714

359766BV00008B/242/P